# MEET YOUR MATE

**Books by Jacie Floyd**

**The Good Riders Series**
MEET YOUR MATE
CURSED BY LOVE
MEANT FOR ME
HAPPY THIS YEAR

**The Billionaire Brotherhood**
WINNING WYATT
DARING DYLAN
REMAKING RYAN

**The Sunnyside Series**
Everybody Knows

# MEET YOUR MATE

AWARD-WINNING AUTHOR
JACIE FLOYD

For Goble, my hero for life.
Everything. Always.

# Chapter One

"And the winner of this year's Community First award is—" Annabel heightened the imaginary suspense with a mental drum roll as she pulled into the local television station's parking lot. Beelining for an empty spot at the end of the row, she allowed hometown favorite George Clooney to announce, "Challenging Destiny, Lasting Productions, Annabel Morgan and Howard Lasting, producers!"

Normally, she only conjured up her favorite career fantasy in dark and private moments, but today she'd paraded it out in bright sunlight to distract herself from a raging case of stage fright. After all, she didn't appear on an afternoon talk show every day. Or in front of a television camera ever. Her nerves were stretched tighter than her budget.

Easing through the tandem parking slot from one side to the other, she pictured herself at the upcoming award ceremony. Dressed to impress in something sophisticated and expensive, she'd step up to accept the award that would change her life. Just as George took her in his arms for a meaningful exchange of glances and a long congratulatory kiss filled with infinite possibilities, a sickening crunch jolted her back to reality.

The front bumper of her ten-year-old Saab was metal-on-metal with a small, flashy vehicle attempting to back into the space she'd been sliding into headfirst.

Grimacing over her carelessness and the certainty of another insurance claim on the heels of her seventeen-year-old stepdaughter's mishap the month before. Annabel shifted her car into park. She clutched the hem of her mini-skirt to keep it from rising to indecent heights as she stepped out to meet her victim. Good thing it was May, not January, or she'd freeze her butt off.

"Hey, lady," a testosterone-laden voice growled over the slam of a car door. "You should keep your mind on your driving when you're behind the wheel."

Fresh from her bout of daydreaming, Annabel bit back the urge to tell the chauvinist where to stick his opinion. She glanced at the slight crease in her fender and the deeper dent in his, relieved that the damage hadn't been worse. Shoulders squared, she turned to exchange info with the other driver and admit her guilt.

Damn. Investigative reporter 'Mad Max' Williams. An apology died on her lips. Even though he worked at the television station, he spent most of his time out on assignment. She'd hoped she wouldn't run into him today. And now she had. Literally.

She crossed her arms and studied him with a chilling look. Professional acquaintances and personal opposites in work habits and lifestyles, he was her biggest rival for the community service award she coveted.

Aside from their award competition, she'd worked with him on several projects for Lasting Productions. Her work involved insignificant details like scriptwriting, casting, editing, and scheduling. His duties included the more challenging tasks of sitting in a booth and recording the voiceover, flirting with female assistants, distracting male interns with assorted hijinks, generally creating chaos, getting paid the big bucks, and receiving most of the recognition.

Everything about his flamboyant image and overbearing self-confidence rubbed her the wrong way. It annoyed her to admit that the broad shoulders and rugged good looks the television camera loved were even more compelling in person than they were on the small screen. But the less-than savory details she'd witnessed and heard about from others prevented her from lusting after the exterior packaging that rivaled Clooney's.

Smoothing down her skirt, she waited for Max's leisurely perusal to move from her new pointy-toed high-heeled shoes and past her uncustomary form-fitting outfit to her face. As expected, the interested gleam dimmed from his eyes and switched to disbelief as recognition kicked in.

"Nice legs, Morgan. First time I've seen you in anything but your Iron Maiden costume. You should show that figure off more often." He lounged against the hood of her car and let his gaze travel her body a second time. "This new look is almost enough to excuse you from rear-ending me. But not quite. What had you so distracted?"

"What do you mean?" Like she'd be willing to share her hopes and dreams with him.

"You sure weren't thinking about your driving, and you couldn't have been preoccupied with your love life since everyone knows you don't have one."

"Whereas you," she countered, poking a finger into his rock-solid chest, "were probably thinking about the bevy of mud wrestlers, rodeo queens, and strippers you're currently dating."

"Hey!" He straightened up with mild indignation. "Candy LaBar's not a stripper. She's an exotic dancer. Her act's very artistic."

Already running late, Annabel didn't have time to trade childish insults with Max. She dismissed the response with a flick of the wrist. "I'll bet."

He whipped his phone out, then took pictures of the damage to both bumpers. As she stepped toward the television station's main entrance, his fingers clamped around her elbow. "Aren't you forgetting something?" He jerked a thumb toward his car. "Damage? Repair? Insurance?"

"It's just a scratch."

He shook his head at her dismissive attitude. "It's just a scratch on the bumper of a vintage Porsche I've spent two years restoring. Whether they fix it or replace the bumper, it's not going to come cheap."

That figured. "I'll have my insurance company contact you."

"They better, or I'll send the repair bill straight to you."

"Fine, fine." Annabel marched forward, eager to leave Mad Max behind. But he fell into step alongside her with his customary swagger.

"By the way," he said, "congratulations on the Community First nomination."

She slid a peek at him from the corner of her eye and examined his comment for sarcasm. His expression remained suspiciously sincere. "You, too."

"Who'd have thought we'd be nominated in the same category?"

"Not me. The mind still boggles over my documentary about inner-city high school students competing with your four-part exposé on botched boob jobs."

"That's one way of describing them," he said before urging, "Just remember what they say."

"What do they say, Max? Sex sells?" Why does he always manage to bring out my inner bitch?

"No-oo. It's an honor just to be nominated."

She coated the smile she turned on him with pure sugar. "You remember that when they call out my name from the podium." She prayed they'd call out her name. Her professional and financial future hinged on winning the award.

"Yeah, right. I've got the award all but in my hands." He raised her show of bravado with an ante of overconfidence.

"And how many judges did you sleep with to make that happen?" The accusation almost shamed her as she made it.

"Talent earns its own reward." A glint of real pride moved behind his dark brown eyes as he veered away from her, toward the news team's entrance. "See ya later, Morgan."

"Not if I see you first," Annabel muttered to his retreating back.

Against her better judgment, she watched him stride masterfully toward the building. Then, he looked over his shoulder and caught her watching him. Lifting her chin, she turned to glide into the main entrance. Her face flushed when she twisted her ankle on the new heels. *Damn, he probably saw that.*

Putting the incident behind her, she hurried into the lobby where Carly waited. Her stepdaughter bounced in anticipation of their joint television appearance. A quick hug went a long way toward banishing Max from Annabel's thoughts and quelling her preshow anxiety. "Been waiting long?"

"Long enough to find out everything we need to know." Excitement widened Carly's bright blue eyes to saucer-size. "First, sign in here, then follow me."

Annabel had visited the station many times and knew her way around, but she allowed the bouncing teen to lead her to the makeup room anyway. After they'd settled into chairs, an energetic elf with purple-streaked hair introduced herself as "Voila!" then set to work. She dabbed foundation on their faces, swiped blush on their cheeks, and applied goop to their eyes.

"Not so much, please." Annabel pushed Voila's hand away. She didn't want to look like a clown, and Carly's fresh appeal didn't need much enhancement.

Voila frowned. "You'll look sickly without it."

"You know she's right, and I want you to look awesome. Please?" Her stepdaughter's coaxing did the trick after the makeup artist's opinion had failed to win Annabel over.

Voila hurried to apply a few finishing touches. Annabel assessed her reflection in the mirror then blotted off a coat of shiny magenta lipstick. She tugged the lapels of her snug teal jacket together. As soon as she released them, they separated into a wide V that exposed the barely-there cleavage created by her new push-up bra.

"I don't know how you talked me into buying this suit. I'm touched by the attempt to update my image, but I have plenty of other, more suitable clothes."

"More boring, you mean." Carly brushed Annabel's hands away from the lapels. "You'll be in front of a camera instead of hiding behind one for a change. You should wear something that makes you look young and hot, instead of old and frigid."

"Let's take your hair down to really boost your image." Voila pulled pins out of the bun at the base of Annabel's neck.

"No." Annabel covered her hair with her hands to keep Voila's busy fingers out of it. "It's too curly and flies around when it's not pulled back."

"Hmmm." Voila cocked her head and considered for a moment before sweeping Annabel's locks into a French twist with just a few loose tendrils. The style softened the angles of her face and enhanced the shape of her light-gray eyes.

If her stepdaughter weren't sitting right there beside her with Carly's own brand of youthful, natural beauty, Annabel wouldn't have recognized herself.

"You look gorgeous," Carly enthused as they made their way to the green room next door. "Super hot!"

"You look fabulous, too." Annabel pulled the girl's long French-braid in front of her shoulder as they stepped into the waiting room. "But we're going on a program to discuss successful stepparent/stepchild relationships. We're not trolling for guys on the internet."

"Close enough," murmured a pencil-thin woman nibbling a carrot stick by the snack table.

As they took seats on a lumpy sofa, Carly refused to meet Annabel's eyes. Never a good sign. Annabel studied the seven other sets of parent/teen duos.

While a couple of parents glanced at her curiously, the

others flicked pitying looks her way. None of the teenagers managed to look her in the eye.

A wary tingle replaced stage fright as the reason for her damp palms. "Close enough to what?"

Before anyone responded, a chipper production assistant buzzed in, wearing a headset and clasping an electronic tablet. "My name's Justine. On behalf of Tess Hartley, I'd like to welcome all of you to *Let's Talk*. We're going to open with the kids on camera. If you'd head that way, please..." She motioned the younger group toward the door. "I'll come back for the parents shortly."

Carly squeezed Annabel's hand. The teenager's excitement fizzed palpably between them like a carbonated cola.

"Good luck, Anna," Carly whispered. "Please don't be mad," she added before slipping away.

*Don't be mad?* That simple plea put Annabel's parental alarm system on full alert. She was all too familiar with the way the high-spirited girl's best intentions frequently misfired. "Mad about what?"

From the doorway, Carly flashed a mischievous smile and escaped with the other teenagers. Except for the gurgle of an espresso machine in the corner, the room swirled with awkward silence. Annabel thought of all the editing waiting for her back at the production studio and longed for the safety of her ordinary routine.

A military-type with ramrod-straight posture and square jaw stopped at the end of the sofa. "When you came in," he said, "I wasn't sure if you were a parent or one of the kids."

The flattery tickled Annabel. Only fourteen years older than Carly, people occasionally guessed they were sisters. But she couldn't imagine anyone mistaking her for a teenager. Maybe the kick-ass outfit Carly chose for her had shaved off some years.

"Stepparent." She glanced around the room, trying to interpret the spike in atmosphere. "Aren't we all?

A couple of "Not me's" mingled with one "I am."

"What's going on here?" she asked GI Joe.

He nodded toward a monitor where the smiling face of Cincinnati's answer to Oprah filled the screen. "Watch and learn."

Tess Hartley let her lively theme song and the audience's applause fade away before she introduced the day's episode.

"Today on *Let's Talk*, we're going to meet a group of caring teens who are concerned about their single parents."

Concerned! The word bounced around inside Annabel's head like a loose basketball on a gym floor. Why would Carly be concerned about her? Discomfort plummeted into downright dread.

"Through death, divorce, or abandonment," Tess continued, "all of these high-school seniors live in single-parent households. As they prepare to leave home for the first time, they worry about their parents' lonely futures. Isn't that sweet?"

Tess's audience agreed with enthusiastic applause, but Annabel didn't think *sweet* accurately described it. In the green room, the knowing nods of some parents and the shocked expressions of others who'd been duped confirmed her assessment.

"Please, join me while they—" Tess paused and gestured for the studio audience to join in the recitation of the show's well-known tag line "—tell Tess about it."

Justine reappeared in the green room, buzzing along just as hyper and efficient as before. But now, she looked more sheepish than capable. "In case you haven't figured it out, some of you are here under false pretenses. There's nothing illegal or unethical going on. The kids are really excited. But if any of you prefer not to participate, you need to let me know now—before we get too far into the taping."

Well, that gave them plenty of leeway. Annabel swallowed hard and found her voice. "What exactly have they gotten us into? A televised ambush?"

"They're playing matchmaker," the anorexic woman said, practically rubbing her hands together in anticipation. "I can't wait to see who I get fixed up with."

"Matchmaker?" Annabel picked up her purse, ready to head for the door.

"That's right," Justine confirmed. "Last week, all of them interviewed potential partners from a pool of prescreened, preapproved applicants. They each handpicked someone for their single parent to go out with on one or two dates arranged by and recorded for a future episode of *Let's Talk*. Their choices are here to meet you today."

"What kind of dates?" Annabel asked.

"Whatever you and your arranged partner want. You'll each

get to name your perfect evening, and the show will foot the bills—within reason. No flying to New York or Paris, but anything local will be fine."

"I plan on going to The Precinct," GI Joe chimed in. Although the steakhouse wouldn't be Annabel's choice, a flurry of laughter and hoots of agreement followed the mention of one of Cincinnati's most expensive restaurants.

"You can decide on your destinations later." Justine's gaze flicked to the clock on the wall and then settled on the monitor. "But you'll need to make up your minds quickly about appearing."

Out in the studio, the camera panned the line of fledgling matchmakers. Just as Annabel opened her mouth to refuse, the camera zeroed in on Carly and focused on her blonde good looks. In that moment, Annabel forgot the trick the girl had played and felt a thrill of pride at her stepdaughter's composure. She glowed as Carly spilled the beans about Annabel.

"She's my stepmom. My dad got custody of me when my biological mother left us. He married Annabel when I was nine, and after he died three years ago, I stayed with her. My birth mom is awesome in a fairy godmother kind of way, but she's not very good with, um, details." A smile curled the corners of Carly's mouth. "Annabel's the one who's always tucked me in, taken me to the dentist, soccer games and piano recitals. You know, all that Mom-and-responsibility stuff."

"Does she work outside the home?" Tess asked.

"Oh, yeah, she's a documentary editor for a local production company. A project she worked on is nominated for some big award." Carly paused before confiding, "She's so proud that I plan to go to medical school eventually, but except for me, her work's all she's got. I'm afraid she'll use it as an excuse not to get a real life after I leave for college next fall."

*Not true!* Annabel had lots of other things and people in her life. *Didn't she?* Hmmm, maybe not.

She cringed as the little blabbermouth ratted her out to the entire tri-state area. Maybe if she'd informed Carly about her plans for the future, this fiasco could have been avoided.

Truthfully, after all the responsibilities she'd handled over the years, Annabel yearned for an exciting, carefree life of her own.

She loved her stepdaughter and enjoyed her company, but

Annabel looked forward to the graduating teen's departure with more anticipation than dread. As soon as Carly left for Ohio State, Annabel planned to cut loose and make her own dreams come true.

Some of her plans involved work goals, sure, but they also included increasing her social life. All right, make that *developing* a social life. With an all-new, daring, and spontaneous attitude, she wanted to flit off to a weekend in Belize… go skydiving… date guys with tattoos.

Since she didn't want Carly feeling as if Annabel itched to get rid of her, she hadn't mentioned any of her secret desires to her stepdaughter. But now Annabel could see the advantages of opening up a bit more. She'd remedy that issue immediately after today's show.

Carly's sweet gesture revealed a misguided need to repay Annabel for her love, and Annabel would never hurt the girl's feelings by refusing the gesture. She considered the possibility of easing herself into her new ready-for-anything persona with two vetted, chaperoned, on-camera dates. *How bad could they be?*

Smothering a sense of impending doom, she summoned her courage long enough to sign the release forms Justine handed to her. Within moments, she found herself taking a deep breath and stepping center stage. Her eyes adjusted to the glaring lights while she waited for her cue.

"Carly took great care in choosing a man who shares common interests with her stepmother. You'll recognize him as WKLK's most popular and handsome investigative reporter. These two already know one another, but let's see if sparks fly when they're paired up for romance." Tess and the camera turned toward Annabel. "*Let's Talk* is pleased to welcome Annabel Morgan and her lucky date, Max Williams!"

The introduction barely registered in Annabel's head before a tall, muscular form bounded out from stage right. He turned her with a hand on her arm and planted a kiss on her check.

Stunned, she reared back to confirm her misfortune. The shock in his eyes mirrored hers.

Under cover of the applause, they objected in unison, "Not you!"

The following Saturday night, Max arrived on Annabel's front porch in Hyde Park. With his favorite cameraman in tow, he looked around at one of Cincinnati's oldest and stodgiest neighborhoods. Sturdy brick houses lined the quiet, residential street. Subdued shutters bordered windows with overflowing flower boxes. Tidy yards sported geometric mower grids. Traditional, conservative, established, and settled. All things Max preferred to avoid.

Grinding his teeth, he cursed his current circumstances and the unapologetic people responsible for it. If given the chance, he'd banish meddlesome teenage girls to a world without cell phones or teenage boys.

He'd blast Tess Hartley to an unending life of flat hair, tabloid journalism, and bad ratings.

He'd send all judgmental, uninteresting women to an island far, far away, where they could bore one another to death with their rules, restrictions, and lack of original thoughts.

And he'd reserve a special circle of hell composed of angry advertisers, prolonged power outages, and drunken weathermen for Charley Asherton, the usually-sensible station manager who had included Max's name in a pool of eligible bachelors for *Let's Talk* without notifying him first.

How he'd let Tess and Charley talk him into participating in such an asinine waste of time, Max couldn't explain. He'd thought it a joke when he received the message to appear for the first-round interviews. But he hadn't stood a chance against the innocent wiles and harmless demeanor of the young girl who singled him out. If he'd known she'd matched him up with Ms. Frostbite of Cincinnati, he would have pulled a no-show for the actual program.

Tess would pay for this. Due to their brief, steam-up-the-sheets, personal history half-a-dozen years ago, he'd expected her to let him out of his arranged date. When a conspiratorial smile and the promise of a future favor hadn't worked, he explained that Annabel didn't want to go out with him any more than he wanted to go out with her.

The ratings-minded diva just laughed and insisted he keep his part of the bargain. She'd even had the nerve to goad him over the fact that he'd finally met a woman who didn't worship at his feet. Tess had also suggested he look on winning Annabel over as a challenge—one the show would pay for and record—

as the "relationship" unfolded. Relationship, hell. Disaster was more like it. And Tess had licked her glossy lips over the possibility.

Ever conscious of the camera, the reporter in Max erased the scowl and put on his game face. He shot the sleeves of his suit into place, then smoothed his hair and straightened his frigging tie.

"Quit primping, Casanova, you look fine," Roger said from behind him. He lifted the video-camera to his eye. "Now, ring the bell. No, wait. The doorknocker seems more forceful, more masculine. Use that."

"More masculine." Max snorted but banged the knocker as instructed. "Masculinity's wasted on Annabel. Why do smart women like her favor those limp-wristed sensitive types who drink lattes and go to poetry readings?"

"Why do you care what kind of men she likes?"

"I don't. I'm just saying, she's not my type."

"Yeah, I can see why the combination of smart, nice, gorgeous, and talented wouldn't work for you," the cameraman muttered.

When the door swung open, Max faced the beaming teenager who'd gotten him into this mess.

"You're here!" Carly clapped her hands.

Despite his annoyance, Max grinned at her enthusiasm. "Hey, kid. How's it going?"

She peered over his shoulder to the street, then leaned out the door to view the driveway. His Jeep Cherokee elicited a frown. "Where's the limo?"

With the Porsche in the shop, he'd been tempted by the station's offer of transportation, but he hated that kind of fancy crap. Besides, he and Annabel weren't two pimply-faced, sweaty-palmed teenagers on the way to the prom. "I prefer to drive myself."

Carly planted her hands on her hips. "But what about what Anna prefers?"

"When we talked yesterday, I asked her if she wanted to show off with a car and driver." He shrugged. "She said she didn't care."

"Well, if you put it that way, what else could she say?" She glared at him with disapproval. "Besides, *I* care. I want this to be so special for her."

"Maybe next time, kid." Of course, there would be no such event. The terms of the show indicated he could dictate when and where they went on their second date, if he wanted to see her again. In a rare moment of agreement, he and Annabel had decided this would be a one-shot deal. She would have to be the one to break the news to Little Ms. Blue Eyes here.

Carly accepted the disappointment with a grudging sigh. "Come on in, then. Anna's almost ready."

He stepped across the threshold of the Morgan home, suppressing the urge to sneeze. The place smelled like a damn flower shop. Fresh roses decorated a table in the foyer. Potpourri sat in little dishes around the living room. They probably even sprayed the air with floral perfume.

In about two minutes, he'd break out in hives from the cloying scent combined with the rampant middle-class-values decor. Family pictures lined the mantle in the living room. Knick-knacks rested on frilly lace things. He'd bet his Porsche that coasters bloomed automatically under every beverage.

Structured, neat, and fragrant, a reflection of Annabel herself.

Everything in the house whispered its good taste in monotonous neutrals. Nice, he supposed, if he went in for this sort of *Boy Meets World*, mom, and apple-pie hominess.

Which he didn't.

Not that he had any reason to dislike sitcom-perfect domesticity. But growing up without a mother present, he'd never experienced it. This whole scene existed as the polar opposite of his childhood and adulthood. Both had teemed with loud and boisterous chaos.

He'd never lived anywhere that remotely resembled this house or neighborhood, and he'd never dated a woman with as little fire and flash as Annabel.

Roger trailed him inside. "Would you go out and come back in again? The lighting in here isn't what I expected."

"Forget it," Max said. "We're not staging anything or doing any retakes."

"If you're willing to settle for a pasty image that makes you look like one of *The Walking Dead*, fine by me."

Annabel's stepdaughter chewed on her thumbnail and creased her forehead as she eyed Roger from head to sneaker. Max empathized with her concerns about the two-hundred-twenty-pound free spirit sporting a ponytail, eyebrow piercing, forearm tattoos, scruffy jeans, and a concert T-shirt. He attempted to set her at ease. "Roger's the chaperone-slash-shooter for tonight. Even though he's misguided enough to worship the Dave Matthews Band instead of real rock 'n' roll, he's harmless when he's not obsessing about things like camera angles and lighting."

"If you say so." Carly took a small step back, as if reluctant to give them the benefit of the doubt. "Please take a seat in the living room. Anna said to offer you something to drink and let her know when you got here."

A footstep at the top of the stairs alerted Max to his date's presence before he could decline the offer. In spite of himself, he watched Annabel descend.

A nervous smile flickered and softened her expression before it dimmed and faded into the more familiar lines of stern disapproval. And he hadn't even done anything to annoy her yet. That he knew of.

Roger stepped forward. He adjusted the camera to zoom in and capture her entrance.

Waiting at the foot of the stairs, Max assessed her appearance. She'd reverted to full-on Ice-Princess mode. Black suit jacket buttoned up to her chin, and skirt hem hanging down past her knees. Sensible, boxy looking shoes. Hair slicked back so tightly at the nape of her neck he was surprised her eyes didn't cross.

"Anna, I thought you were going to wear your hair down." Carly's artless comment inserted a drop of sweetness into the awkward moment.

Annabel smoothed her fingers over the sides of her hair, as if to harness any rebellious strands that dared to escape from their prison. "I'm more comfortable with it up."

"You look gorgeous." Roger panned the camera between the woman and girl. He nudged Max in the ribs, then pulled back to record Max and Annabel's first greeting. "Doesn't she look gorgeous? Give her a little kiss."

Max's gaze skimmed over Annabel's body again. The classy, understated style suited her. *Too prim and proper for my taste.* Although the suit did hug her figure nicely. The slit up one side of her skirt showed an enticing bit of shapely leg and thigh when she walked. And that mouth with the peek-a-boo smile playing around the edges almost begged for a kiss.

But the expression of alarm that crossed her face sure didn't. Or the backpedaling she employed as he reached for her.

"Oh, my." She fluttered her fingers like crazed bats. "I guess I'm not very good on this side of the camera."

"Just pretend I'm not here," Roger said as if it would be possible to overlook a supersized gorilla with a forty-thousand-dollar camera glued to his face.

"Then quit trying to direct everything," Max told him. "Just let things happen. And don't worry," he said to Annabel. "I'll make him stay ten paces behind us at all times."

"No, no, he's fine. He's just doing his job. Getting a taste of my own medicine will make me more sympathetic to my subjects in the future." She flashed the cameraman an elusive smile.

She excluded Max from the offering of goodwill. Okay, he got the message. He shoved his hands in his pockets. "You ready to go?"

"Yes." She turned to retrieve some kind of flimsy wrap from the closet. "Do you know where we're going?"

"Nope. I was only told where and when to show up—and what to wear." He pulled at the knot on his necktie again. Damn thing. He hated having to wear one on his day off.

"We have a reservation at Ernesto's at six."

*Ernesto's.* The kind of restaurant Max tended to dodge. A stuffy, over-priced, pretentious place in Mt. Adams that served prissy little portions of nouvelle cuisine. Sighing, he resigned himself to the choice and tried not to yawn.

"From there, we'll go to the symphony. I hope you like Wagner."

He chuckled, assuming she was kidding. But when he checked, her expression revealed nothing but seriousness. "Wagner? Really?"

"His music's quite stimulating. My husband and I used to have season tickets for the symphony. I gave them up when he—" She stopped and bit her lip. "I gave them up a few years ago."

The symphony. Stimulating? Ri-ight. She must be older than he guessed. What decade had she been born in anyway? Oh, well, maybe he could catch up on his sleep.

And he'd given up his poker night for this.

# Chapter Two

Since the camera recorded and magnified every emotion, Annabel attempted to hide her irritation from the high-powered lens hovering a few feet away. She glanced toward Max on the other side of the table and found herself viewing only the menu propped up against the floral centerpiece.

She didn't need to see him in his flawless Italian suit to know he looked sinfully delicious. His rugged physique, gorgeous face, and observant eyes oozed sensuality—damn him—in that casual, devil-may-care way of his. But as her mother used to say, "Handsome is as handsome does."

And so far, Max's behavior had resembled a toad's.

From his outrageous reputation with women, she'd expected more charm. He'd remained almost mute on the ride over. She wasn't exactly thrilled to be on this date either, but at least *she* tried to be pleasant.

"What looks good?" she said, just to break the silence.

Max closed the menu and dropped it on the table before tucking his cell phone into his inside suit pocket. "Sorry, did you say something?"

He'd been texting someone or checking his messages? What an insensitive jerk! She sniffed back her disapproval. "I asked you what looks good."

"The exit," he muttered.

Offended even further, Annabel's spine straightened automatically. "What?"

"Sorry, again." He stuck a finger in his collar and pulled it away from his neck. "This isn't my kind of place."

Candles and ferns, crisp white linens and gleaming crystal filled the room. Music from a harpist in the corner drifted around them and enhanced the cool ambience of the pale green and silver decor. The overall effect was lovely and—in the right company—very romantic, but Max's grimace spoke volumes about his disapproval.

"Oh, right." She leaned forward and tried to produce a

sincere-looking smile. "I guess you'd be more comfortable in some smoke-filled dive with peanut shells on the floor and a runway for strippers."

"That does sound appealing." His eyes lit up before he shrugged in resignation. "But I'd settle for a menu that's written in English and a meal that won't leave me hungry five minutes after it's over."

Annabel nodded with feigned sympathy. "I considered making a reservation at one of those places that sizzle up plate-sized sirloins while you graze at a salad bar with fifteen different kinds of bean and Jell-O concoctions. But then, I remembered this was supposed to be *my* dream date, not yours."

"You got that right."

Stung by his disapproval, her defenses rose along with her temper. "Listen, buddy, this debacle is as much your fault as mine. After the show the other day, *you* said you could get us out of this deal."

He spread his hands wide. "I tried."

"Not hard enough."

"Hey, you could have refused, too."

True, she could have. But when she saw Carly's bright eyes, thrilled with the success of fixing her up with one of the best-looking, most-famous guys in town, the girl's excitement held her back. Annabel bit her lip to keep from bursting her stepdaughter's bubble by revealing that Mad Max Williams was as well-known for his off-camera escapades as for his news reporting. Some of the gossip that swirled around him could be dismissed, but not all of it. Not when Annabel had glimpsed the results of his deplorable behavior firsthand.

She took a deep breath and reined in her annoyance, silently repeating her chant of the past week. *It's just one date.* And to be fair, Max had explained when they'd talked on the phone that he'd been suckered into the gig, too.

A starchy waiter materialized beside them, drawing Annabel's attention away from her personal dilemma and back to the meal.

"Are you ready to order?" Starch asked in nasal tones.

"Ladies first." Max waved his hand toward her.

Annabel's stomach growled. Obviously, skipping lunch had been a mistake. She ordered bruschetta with a gorgonzola tapenade, Greek salad, risotto with caramelized pumpkin and chorizo along with glazed Mediterranean vegetables.

"Very good, madam. And for you, sir?"

Max frowned. "I know what I *don't* want."

"And what would that be?" Starch narrowed his eyes down a long nose at Max. *He probably doesn't get that look of disapproval pointed at him very often.*

"I don't want anything bruschetta, frittata, polenta or Florentine."

Starch sniffed as he gathered the menus and tucked them under his arm. "Might I recommend the New York strip steak *without* the piquant Pepper Coulis that normally accompanies it?"

"That sounds more like it." Max rubbed his hands together in anticipation. "Rare with a shot of hot sauce, a baked potato, plenty of sour cream, and a house salad with ranch dressing."

Pokering up even more, Starch gestured toward Roger at the next table. "And for the other gentleman?"

"You want the same?" Max asked.

The cameraman held up his ham-sized hand, then pointed at Max before answering. "The station's paying, right?"

Max nodded. "Yep, live large."

Roger's gleeful smile exposed a mischievous dimple. "If the steaks are less than ten ounces each, I'll have two."

"Very good, sir." With a small patronizing bow, Starch faded away from the table.

After a moment's silence, Annabel ventured a new topic. "Has my insurance company contacted you about fixing your car yet?"

"Yep, I'll have the Porsche back by Tuesday." He leaned forward, warming to the subject. "I got three appraisals, but they approved my first choice. A buddy of mine from—"

He stopped mid-sentence as a new presence appeared between them. At Max's right elbow, a sommelier cradled a towel-wrapped bottle of champagne. The sober-faced young man with his longish hair slicked back, a soul patch, and wire-rimmed glasses set flutes in front of them. Glancing at Max, the sommelier did a double take.

"Hey, dude, aren't you Max Williams?" He unbent with an enthusiasm that contradicted the waiter's steely behavior. "I've been following that story you broke last month about the county parks commissioner skimming funds. My wife used to work for the parks department and she always said there was something fishy going on. They fired her for being a squeaky wheel. Now, that it's more than just her word against theirs, maybe she'll get her job back."

"I hope she does." Max transformed himself into his outgoing public persona and shook the sommelier's outstretched hand. "Keep me posted, okay? I might do a follow-up."

"I'll do that. Could I get your autograph? My wife will never believe I met you. You're her hero."

"Sure, what's your name?" He squinted to read the nametag in the dim light. "Alvin, right? You want me to sign this to you or your wife?"

Watching Max scribble his signature across a wine list, Annabel wasn't sure if Alvin or the Dom Perignon would bubble over first. The sommelier sobered into business-like demeanor after the maitre d' reappeared and signaled him to get on with business. Alvin expertly uncorked the bottle and poured. Max conducted the ritual tasting with a frown, then said something to Alvin in an undertone. The sommelier nodded and bowed himself away.

Annabel eyed the champagne. She hadn't tasted any since her wedding night eight years ago. She hadn't much liked it then. "Who ordered this?"

"Not me. I can't stand the stuff. I asked Alvin to bring me a scotch."

"I ordered it," Roger piped up from behind his camera. "I want a shot of you two clinking glasses. The bubbles make an interesting effect in the candlelight. Raise your glasses and make a toast, Max."

Annabel expected him to refuse or ignore the direction, the way he had with the kiss. But without further prompting, he held his flute aloft. "Congratulations on the Community First nomination. May the best project win."

She raised her glass. "I'll drink to that."

They clinked and sipped. The Dom tasted crisp and refreshing. Annabel sipped again.

"Have you seen any of the other entries?" he asked in the first unsolicited comment he'd made since they'd been seated.

"They're pretty good."

"But not as good as ours." He smiled. Charismatic, but smug.

She hoped to deflate his ego a little. "Not as good as *mine*."

He didn't make a sound, but the squaring of his shoulders revealed her comment had hit a nerve. "Why is yours the best?"

She sipped her drink and let the bubbles dance around her mouth. Amazing how something so fizzy managed to slide down her throat so smoothly. She sipped again, mentally reviewing the competition. "Randall's entry is about cleaning up the river. It's good, but a similar topic won last year. I don't think this one's good enough to repeat."

One of Max's long, lean fingers circled the rim of his glass. "Same thing about Harris's piece on police brutality."

Annabel nodded. "The dark horse is Lynn Dorey's entry on the Arts' Commission. She came up with a fresh angle on that, and she's got a solid reputation."

"No more solid than yours at Lasting Productions."

Flustered by the unexpected compliment, she reached for her champagne flute again and found it empty. Without waiting for her to ask, Max refilled her glass.

"If yours is the best, and Lynn's is next, where do you rank mine?" Max nodded his thanks as Alvin placed a scotch on the rocks in front of him, then delivered a beer to the cameraman.

"I wish I could rank it last, but you're the big name on the slate. It's impossible to discount you. The station you work for carries a lot of clout, too."

"But you don't think much of my report?" Despite the seeming ease he exhibited while sipping his drink, his eyes glinted at her darkly.

She felt more comfortable with him and thirstier by the minute. "I don't consider it as *weighty* as the others."

"What are you basing your opinion on?"

"The tit-illating subject matter?" She winced over the terrible pun.

"I see. The topics of breast reduction and implant surgery don't meet your high standards." His eyes definitely flashed in the glow of the candles. "A subject doesn't have to be boring or dull to be important, you know."

She was surprised he seemed as defensive of his work as she would be if he belittled hers. From his reputation, she'd assumed his interest lay in the publicity or the acclaim, not the achievement. *Had she judged him unfairly?*

"Aside from boosting your station's sweeps ratings, what were the benefits of your piece for Cincinnati?" she asked.

"That's the yardstick the panel of judges use to select the winner."

"It caused the butcher performing botched surgeries to lose his medical license, and it convinced a jury to convict him of malpractice." Max's intensity revealed his satisfaction in the accomplishment.

Her conscience twitched for underestimating his project as her heart sank. She moved his entry up a notch, even though she still doubted his motives. "But mostly you did it so you could interview exotic dancers, right?"

"Of course. For my money, there aren't nearly enough stories on the news about strippers." One side of his perfect mouth turned up in a self-derogatory smile. "What about yours?"

"*Challenging Destiny* follows twenty promising students through four years at an inner-city high school. We documented their relative success at surviving the pitfalls they faced on a daily basis, everything from gangs and drug abuse to poverty and questionable SAT scores."

"I'm familiar with the premise." He settled back in his chair. "What's the long-range impact?"

"The United Way is using *Challenging Destiny* in its pledge drive this year." Her attempt at modesty failed as her cheeks warmed with pride and her smile stretched wide. "And our state representative showed it to the Ways and Means Committee to request an increase in the education budget for latchkey programs."

He pursed his lips in a low whistle. "Impressive." He clinked his glass with hers again. "That should wow the judges."

"I hope so." Looking down, she discovered her appetizer. When had that arrived? *Starch was a sneaky little snob, wasn't he?* She scooped up a bruschetta and bit off a corner. "Would you like a piece?"

"Maybe later." He smiled and plucked a breadstick out of the basket. Nipping off a crunchy end, he chewed it with relish. Apparently he ate with full-on enjoyment, the same way he did everything.

"I'll have one of those funky tomato things," Roger said to Annabel.

She pulled her gaze away from Max's and offered the plate to the cameraman. "Help yourself."

Finishing off one bruschetta, she reached for another. The salty olive and anchovy spread increased her thirst, and she detoured toward her glass. Tapenade and champagne paired for a wonderful combination, she discovered.

"Why does winning mean so much to you?" Max propped his chin on a fist.

Avoiding his eyes, which seemed entirely too knowing, she dropped her gaze to his tie. If required to describe the entwining pattern on the silk fabric as a Rorschach test, she'd say the two spiraling peach stripes against a charcoal background resembled slender lovers in the night. Very erotic. Almost X-rated. She blinked and focused on his question.

"*You* may have won a lot of professional awards, but I haven't." The temperature in the room must have raised a few degrees. She fingered the top button on her jacket. "As a mom working part-time and a lowly documentary editor, it's not unusual for me to be brought in during post-production. You know my boss Howard Lasting, right? He indicated winning Community First will improve my chances for developing other projects. With Carly going off to college, I plan to devote more time to my career. And increasing my income wouldn't hurt either. I'd love a promotion to fulltime producer."

Annabel stopped and sipped, determined to halt the nonstop stream of words before she revealed anything more intimate or personal. *The champagne must be the reason for this motor mouth tendency.* She imagined his ridicule if she expressed her secret desire to someday work as a producer for an investigative news team. That would give him personal knowledge of her that she just didn't trust him to have in his hands.

Suddenly she felt much too warm and too aware of the dawning interest in the depths of his dark, watchful eyes. As she took another sip of the Dom, she unfastened the top button of her jacket.

Their salads came and went almost without notice. Suddenly, the waiter whisked away the empty plates and presented their entrees with a flourish. Hers, a visual masterpiece of colors and textures. His, a butchered, broiled, carnivorous display. Alvin, bless him, also reappeared bearing another bottle of champagne.

Unprompted, Max refilled her glass and encouraged her to raise it for another toast. "To a better understanding between us.

We're halfway there."

"To a better understanding." She ignored the little tingle shivering down her spine when her gaze met the challenge in his. *A better understanding of what? Halfway where?* Neither of them wanted to be anything more than the wary acquaintances they'd always been. *Did they?* Absolutely not.

Annabel remembered too clearly comforting her friend DeeDee as she sobbed her eyes out, ballooned with pregnancy, after he'd dropped her a couple of years ago. And then there were rumors about a young intern who'd left the station under mysterious and undisclosed circumstances. The station management hushed it up, but speculation abounded that Max had caused the college student's dismissal. The creep.

"Do you remember my friend DeeDee?" She watched and waited for an emotional response.

"DeeDee?" He sipped his scotch and appeared to test the name on his tongue along with the Johnnie Walker's. Squinting, he avoided looking her in the eyes.

"Yes, DeeDee Stevens. She's working in Kansas City now."

"Nice girl," he said, neutrally. "Good news market."

"She has a little boy." Oops, the comment sounded a bit more direct than she intended.

"Does she? I knew she was knocked up when she left town."

"You don't know anything else about it, Mr. Sensitive?" She waited breathlessly for his response. "I thought you two dated for a while."

He shrugged his shoulders. "Flash in the pan. We shared some laughs at a time when she was figuring out what she really wanted."

"Like, a father for her baby?"

"Like that," he said, shrugging again. "It didn't have anything to do with me."

The lukewarm denial left her wanting something more definitive. "Didn't it?"

"Hold on," Roger interrupted before she figured out how to get more out of Max. "I want you both to raise your champagne glasses. Then, Annabel, you circle your arm through his before you take a drink. You know, like they do in wedding pictures."

She bent her arm and followed the instructions. She and Max leaned closer. He smelled even more spicy and delicious than her dinner. "Are you interested in having children?"

Max sputtered and reared back. "Whoa, there, Morgan! Don't go getting any ideas. There's not really a wedding in our future."

Roger groaned over the ruined shot. "Do it again. This time, lock glances and lean into one another like you mean it."

Annabel tried to put some heat into her gaze, but the look probably came across as irritation more than desire. Shifting closer to him, she whispered, "Get over yourself, Williams. I just wondered if a guy like you has any little ones tucked away somewhere." *Like Kansas City.*

For Roger's benefit, Max gave her a smile seductive enough to melt her strongest defenses, but he answered through gritted teeth. "No, I don't."

"Honestly?" She swept her eyelashes downward and processed the response. He sounded sincere but looked annoyed.

"Trust me." He nuzzled her ear. His breath brushed her neck. "I'd *never* walk away from a child."

Breathing in his scent, she wanted to snuggle into him, surrounding herself with his heat and strength. But she hesitated. He'd been vague about his relationship with DeeDee. His reputation insisted he was a jerk with women, albeit a gorgeous, charming, seductive jerk. The most dangerous kind.

"So." Opting to play it safe, she straightened in her seat. The tension evaporated with the staged moment. They returned their attention to their meals. "About the award. Why do *you* want to win?"

He looked up and gave her the mocking version of his trademark smile. "Just to keep you from getting it." He raised and lowered his eyebrows at her in a 'How about that?' gesture that almost made her laugh.

"Tell me the truth," she urged. "You want it, too. As much as I do. I can tell."

His hand stalled over the strip of beef he'd just sliced. "Are we still talkin' about the award, darlin'?" True to form, his Southern accent came out full force when he teased or flirted with the opposite sex. Not that he directed it her way very often.

Her temperature spiked a notch. Without a doubt, she simply had to undo another button or faint from heat stroke. He's a womanizer and a jerk, *remember?*

"Yes," she answered after a too-long pause. "Be serious."

"You're serious enough for both of us." Since it was the truth, the quiet observation didn't sound nearly as insulting as it could have.

"Old news." She tossed his comment aside with a flick of her fingers. "But really, about you…"

He straightened his shoulders and put down his fork. "Winning might polish up my image."

Hmmm, she thought he had the exact image he'd earned. Hard-driving, relentless reporter. Rowdy bad-boy. "You're the leading reporter of the most highly-rated news team in town with a reputation for pursuing a story until you've exposed every sordid detail. Your style may not suit my taste, but no one doubts your professional integrity. But your personal image could use some scrubbing up."

"According to my agent, winning this kind of community service award would benefit both."

She paused to think about that. *What was she missing?* "Why would you care?"

"I'd care if I wanted to leave the market."

It took real effort to keep her mouth from dropping open. The information he'd casually lobbed her way would make a hell of a scoop. And it might very well mean there was an upcoming opening at his station. How many reporters did she know who would kill for a shot at Max's job? "Are you *planning* on leaving Cincinnati?"

For a moment, he looked taken aback, then he shrugged again. "You didn't hear it from me."

"I won't say a word." She had the childish impulse to put her fingers to her lips and pretend to turn a key.

"If I hear any rumors," he warned, "I'll know where they came from."

"Not me," she said.

"Or me," Roger added.

"Damn!" Max clapped a hand to his forehead. "How did I forget a giant like you was sitting there recording all this?"

"Nah, except for that toast, I quit recording when the entrée arrived. Footage of people chewing is never attractive."

*Except for Max. He chews rather well.* Clearly, his superior chewing ability was lost on Roger. She concentrated on making sure she didn't give voice to that opinion.

"Plus," Max said, "*you* hate to miss a meal, even for the sake of your art."

"That, too." Roger finished off his second steak and swiped his napkin across his mouth. "Especially when the station's paying. Do we have time for dessert?"

"Do we? It's—It's—" Annabel squinted to focus on the blurry hands of the diamond-encrusted watch Carl had given her on their wedding day. She didn't remember the numbers being this tiny before. Bringing her wrist closer to her eyes, she then pushed it farther away, certain she could see better with a different angle and better lighting.

Where had the time gone? Between eating, drinking, and conversation, they now lagged way behind schedule.

"We're late! If we leave now, we might make the symphony at intermission." Lurching to her feet, she grabbed hold of Max's arm as she toppled into his lap. His arms slid around her waist and he pulled her close. Annabel longed to stay where she was, to see what would happen next, but the look of interest in his eyes sent her head spinning. Confused, she jumped up. "Come on! We have to hurry."

Max sat beside Annabel front and center in the darkened Music Hall with something she'd call "Wagnerian" booming about them. The music didn't suck too badly after all. It boomed and reverberated at a pulsing and relentless volume. The musicians suffused the notes with more power and emotion than Max would have expected a stage full of stuffed shirts to produce.

On the way over, he'd nearly run a red light at Annabel's urging. The only interruption to her concern about missing the first half of the program was her speculation about what music would be presented in the second. He'd pushed the speed limit and imagined her trim body naked just to keep his eyes from glazing over with boredom.

If someone had asked for his opinion on classical music earlier tonight, he would have assumed they meant classic rock or early Elvis. This richness, this invigorating experience that filled the air around Max and set his pulse pounding existed beyond his normal musical boundaries.

The closest he'd ever come to being carried away by music

before was in the living room back home in Nashville when his dad played guitar and harmonized with Max's two sisters. That always got to him, but in a different way.

The orchestra moved into a rousing piece that he recognized from an old Coppola movie. Annabel leaned against him and he turned to share the bit of cinematic trivia with her. Her head landed on his shoulder. Her long eyelashes shadowed her cheeks, her lips parted slightly.

She'd fallen asleep!

Too much champagne, apparently. Maybe he should have monitored her intake. But, hey. He was nobody's father, she wasn't getting behind the wheel of a car, and she was definitely old enough to know her own limit.

He'd noticed and encouraged the way she'd loosened up after the first glass, but he hadn't realized how tipsy she'd gotten until she'd giggled over the third refill. It turned out that a giggling and tipsy Annabel charmed his socks off.

The excited flush of her cheeks, the tendrils of hair escaping their pins and curling playfully along her jaw, the gleam of hope in her eyes as they discussed the award, all had him wondering what other surprises she concealed under her buttoned-down, look-but-don't-touch facade. Damned attractive, even though she clearly didn't have a high opinion of him or his reputation—personal or professional.

Of course, he could have done more to change her opinion, but what was the point? She'd obviously made up her mind about him a long time ago, and he'd have to reveal other people's secrets to make her change it now.

He smiled and took advantage of the current situation, putting his arm around her and pulling her close. Breathing deeply, he inhaled her enticing scent, lightly sweet and baby fresh. Nothing overtly sexual, cloying or artificial for Annabel, of course, just the pull of something refreshingly honest and temptingly off-limits.

She snuggled into him, her upper body nestled against his, oblivious of her actions. The long skirt with the high-rise slit twisted beneath her, revealing one pleasing limb from ankle to hip. The three buttons she'd undone on her jacket gaped open, exposing the swell of a breast and the hint of red lace.

*Well, well, well.* Who would have expected Annabel Morgan to sport red lace undies?

He shifted in his seat, heating up. Annabel squirmed, too, bringing her arm across his chest and curling her hand around his neck. Her soft breath teased his ear, in-out, in-out, in soundless counterpoint to the orchestra.

The volume, the tone, and the urgency of the notes swelled and increased around him, heavy with promise, building to a crescendo, and begging for a conclusion. His body responded to Annabel and the music with equal escalation.

A fanfare, a flourish, an abrupt silence preceded thunderous applause. The appreciative audience leapt to its feet with shouts of "Bravo" and "More, more."

As if on cue, Annabel's hand dropped to his crotch.

Max remained glued to his seat.

Suddenly, her eyelids fluttered open. She jerked her head from his shoulder, and they stared at one another, nose to nose. The confusion cleared from her eyes while shock drained her cheeks of color. Straightening her spine, she snatched her hand away as if scorched.

He let his smile spread as she settled her rigid dignity around her like a full-metal jacket. She stood up, pulled her jacket into place with an efficient snap, straightened her skirt, and applauded with the others.

Max rearranged his junk and climbed gingerly to his feet.

After they waited through what seemed like a curtain call for every frigging individual member of the orchestra, the lights went up and the crowd crept out sedately. Max held onto Annabel's elbow to prevent her from slipping away.

"Roger didn't want us to leave in the first crush," he reminded her.

"Oh, right." She opened the ridiculously small black purse she clutched like a lifeline. "I probably need to make some repairs before facing the camera again." After retrieving a mirror, she reached up to smooth the sides of her hair, but he clasped her wrist.

"Don't," he said as her pulse beat double-time beneath his fingertips. Interesting. He twined a wisp of hair around his finger and let it spring back into place. "You look sexy like this. Approachable. Touchable."

She pulled her hand away and hid it behind her back. "Wh-Wh-Where—" She cleared her throat. "Where did Roger say to meet him?"

"He said to wait here."

She nodded again, looking at the stage, then the ceiling, and finally, the doors. At everything but him. "How did you like the performance?"

"Very stimulating." He winked. "Was it good for you, too?"

Annabel leaned against the Jeep's headrest as Max pulled into her driveway. Through the open moon roof, thousands of stars sparkled against the dark velvety sky. She pretended to study them while she scrambled to locate the shreds of her composure.

A flash of light in the rearview mirror announced Roger's arrival behind them.

Max shifted the car into park and shut off the motor. She sensed more than saw him turn toward her. In a slick maneuver, he slid his arm across the back of her seat. "I'll tell you the truth."

His fingers tom-tommed against the leather headrest, sending a thundering drumbeat through her temples. Realizing he wasn't going to tell her the truth or anything else until she responded, she turned toward him. "About what?"

"Going into it, I expected this date to be a complete waste, but I had a good time." He begrudged every word, she could tell.

She licked her dry lips. "Even the symphony?"

"*Especially* the symphony." His voice was laced with humor and something deeper. Darker. Desire, maybe? No, probably not.

Mortified all over again, she covered her blushing cheeks with her palms and peeked at him through her fingers. "I'm so sorry about that. It was bad enough to fall asleep, but to—to—" She could hardly bring herself to think about it, let alone say it. "To practically *grope* you in public was totally inappropriate."

She groaned at the recollection of *waking up* from a highly erotic dream in the middle of Music Hall draped across his hard, muscular body with about as much class and subtlety as a cheap one-night stand. She could imagine her late oh-so-proper college professor husband's outrage if she'd let her hand drift across *his crotch* in public. Carl would have flat out stiffened—and not in a sexual way—and pushed her away.

"Aw, don't worry about it. Appropriate behavior is highly overrated." He leaned closer and rubbed his fingertips along the edge of her collar. "You need to lighten up, Morgan. Have some fun."

His touch only grazed her skin occasionally, too infrequently for her to object, just often enough for her to notice... and anticipate. A little too much anticipation for comfort. She batted his hand away like a mosquito.

"Besides, Music Hall was a real educational experience for me. I didn't know you classy, high-brow types went in for public displays of affection." His deep chuckle was rich with infectious amusement.

After maintaining a stiff upper lip for all of two seconds, a chuckle burst free, and she laughed along with him. She had to. Her parents had raised her to conduct herself with the utmost propriety at all times. Her husband expected the same. Most of the people she knew would have been appalled by her behavior tonight. But if Max didn't take her *faux pas* seriously, how could she?

As the laughter died between them, a large form loomed outside the car. Roger! She'd forgotten all about him.

He tapped on the window. "You two heading to the door anytime soon, or should I go get a snack and come back?"

"We're going in now." Max turned and gave Annabel a crooked smile. "The watchful eye of *Let's Talk* awaits. Let's get this over with." He opened his car door. "Wait right there. I want Roger to document an example of my best manners."

Under normal circumstances, she probably wouldn't have obeyed an order from him, but her cellphone dinged. She checked the text message in case of a Carly emergency. But no, just an update on the girl's evening. *Just left movies with Jenna. Home by 12. C U then.*

As she dropped the phone back in her purse, Max opened the door. After years of enjoying similar courtesies from her husband, it seemed only fair to accept this small, but sweet gesture from Max.

When he helped her out of the car, his hand felt warm and strong. Carl's hands had been so frail before he died, so cold. With a stab of betrayal over the comparison, she could barely remember a time when Carl's touch had felt this vital, this supportive. The essential feelings of safety and belonging she'd treasured from him during their courtship had faded after their marriage. They'd evaporated completely with the onset of his illness.

Max kept her hand as they walked to the door, turning to clasp both of hers after they stepped onto the small porch.

"You purposely picked a date you didn't think I'd like, didn't you?"

"Maybe... partly..." She chewed her bottom lip. "Yes."

"I fooled you by having a good time anyway." He put that Southern drawl on and off like a pair of sunglasses, flattening his vowels and stringing out his words with several extra syllables. "Turnabout's fair play, don't you think?"

"What?" Apparently, the champagne had covered her brain in pink fuzz balls, leaving her more than a little slow on the uptake.

"I mean, maybe we should—"

"Are you two going to kiss or not?" Roger interrupted.

Darn Roger, anyway. Why couldn't he keep his mouth shut? What had Max been about to say? Would he have tried to kiss her without being prompted? Would she have let him?

"If you're only going to shake hands, do it, so I can leave. If you're going to kiss, I'll wait around."

"We're *not* going to kiss," Annabel said.

"Yes, we are," Max contradicted. "Get the camera ready, Roger."

# Chapter Three

The fleeting brush of Max's lips against hers came and went before Annabel objected or responded. Not that she could have responded before the tingling after-effects froze her in place.

"Is that the best you can do?" Roger goaded.

"No, I can do better. Want to see?" Max proceeded to show them—and potentially all the people in the tri-state viewing area—exactly how much better he could do.

Even knowing the display was all for show, his arms around her felt too muscular. His mouth on hers felt too possessive. His chest against hers felt all too real. Her eyelids fluttered, then closed. Heat curled through her, warming her from her fingertips to her toes. And in all the interesting places in between.

Had anyone ever kissed her this way before?

Not the much-older husband who treated her with too-much respect even before he got sick. Not the inexperienced boyfriend who dumped her in high school when caring for her mother had taken up so much of her time. Not the sweet, but earnest young artist who had been the only one to show any interest in her since her husband's death.

Desire overcame her resistance to Max's bold kiss. His scotch-flavored tongue flirted with hers. Intoxicated by him more than the champagne, her hands moved up the smooth texture of his suit to grasp his broad shoulders. His hands caressed her, moving down her back to her waist, to her hips, to her—

*Whoa there, buddy! Far enough!*

They each recognized the rapidly escalating level of intimacy at the same moment. Dazed, Annabel took a step back and banged into the door. Max took a step back and teetered off-balance on the edge of the porch. His arms flailed against the inevitable until gravity won the battle.

A freshly blooming azalea bush broke his fall, but he bounced off it and crash-landed in the tulips. A string of curses colored the air.

"Are you all right?" She peered down at him, trying not to laugh.

"I'm fine." His voice came out in that clipped way men have when refusing to admit to any pain less severe than a compound fracture or a bullet wound. He scrambled up and brushed pink petals, leaves, and mulch off his formerly immaculate suit.

"Very smooth. A perfect end to a perfect evening." Roger chuckled from the sidewalk. "Very cinematic. I think I've seen the Three Stooges do something similar, Max. I loved it."

"If you try to use that on the show," Max said, genially, "I'll tie you up, weight you down, and throw you in the river."

Roger waved in Annabel's direction. "Then give me something better."

"With pleasure..." Max advanced up the porch steps again.

Annabel held up her hands to ward him off, but blinked at the heat and determination banked in his eyes. She braced herself for her third kiss of the night—making it a record number for the last three years.

Her heart fluttered with pleasure, then fear. She reacted to the second instead of the first and took charge. She straight-armed him to a stop. "Hold it, right there."

His eyebrows shot up. "What?"

"*I'll* do it."

He spread his arms wide and awarded her with a devilishly tempting smile. "Be my guest, babe."

Gripping his shoulders, Annabel rose up on tiptoe and brushed her mouth against his. She gave him a reasonable, respectable, acceptable kiss. Not long, not short, not wet, a little dry actually, but heck, she barely knew him. And what she did know about him she'd never liked, except for tonight. And tomorrow, she would blame her brief change of heart on the champagne, remembering in great detail his many unlikable qualities.

She ignored the goose bumps his hands produced as they caressed her sides, the way his lips clung to hers as she pulled away, and the disappointment that replaced the heat in his eyes.

"Did you get that?" she asked Roger, unable to tear her gaze away from Max's.

"Every brief and boring second," he grumbled. "Is that really the one you want me to use?"

"Yes, please." Taking Max's right hand in hers, she pumped it with business-like detachment. "You've now fulfilled your commitment to me, Carly, Tess and *Let's Talk*. Thank you for a lovely evening."

He shrugged. "You'll have a honker of a headache in the mornin'. Take something for it before you go to bed. And drink lots of water."

"I will." She swallowed back the comments hovering on her tongue. To say anything more would be pointless. If she hung on to restraint for a few more seconds, he'd be gone from her life for good, except as the peripheral irritant he'd always been. "Good night."

"'Night, Morgan." His hands slid into his pockets, his jaw tensed, and yet he stayed. *Waiting for me to go inside.* Even though he hailed from the South, she hadn't expected him to behave like such a Southern gentleman. She opened the door with a cautious backward glance and stepped into her foyer.

She closed the door firmly against Max and any crazy desires he'd stirred up inside her. Disappointment settled around her. "And that's the end of my one and only date with Mad Max Williams."

The peculiar echoing silence of an empty house confirmed Carly's absence. Annabel made her way from foyer to kitchen, setting aside her purse, kicking off her shoes, and pulling pins from her hair. She gave her scalp a vigorous massage while she checked the clock. Ten till twelve. Carly would be home soon.

Upstairs, Annabel had finished brushing her teeth when the teenager framed herself in the bathroom door.

With bright and eager eyes, she probed for details. "How was it? Tell me everything. When did you get home? Did he come in for coffee? Did he kiss you goodnight?"

"It was fine. *He* was fine." Annabel reached into her medicine chest for the bottle of Advil. "I had a nice time."

"Oh, no." Carly groaned. "How bad was it?"

Annabel washed the capsules down with water. "It was fine, I told you."

"Did he laugh too loud? Talk with his mouth full? Make stupid jokes? Snore during the concert?"

Annabel laughed at the deluge of questions. Carly often came into her room for date post-mortems, but this time they'd switched roles. The date under discussion was hers, not her daughter's. Weird. "None of the above. Why do you assume the worst?"

"You're not taking regular aspirin, you're taking extra-strength," Carly pointed out. "He must have done something horrible to give you a headache."

"It's preventive medicine." Annabel slipped a comfy flannel robe on over her favorite *Lord of the Rings* nightshirt. "I drank too much champagne."

"You?" Carly gaped as they moved into the bedroom. "You always preach moderation. You never even finish a glass of wine." The girl plopped herself in the middle of Anna's bed and crossed her legs Indian-style. Moving a stack of folded laundry aside that Carly had brought up earlier, Annabel sat in the overstuffed chair in the corner. "Don't tell me he was trying to get you drunk! That's so juvenile."

"Oh, I don't think so." Annabel pulled her feet under her and considered the idea. "He didn't order the champagne. The cameraman did. Besides, what would Max's motive have been? We had a chaperone, after all."

"Oh, right, the incredible hulk." Carly made a face. "That must have been like when I was in junior high. You'd take me and Tommy Dent to the movies and sit in the row behind us."

"Except I didn't train a camera on you or tell you how to pose the whole time."

The corners of Carly's mouth turned up in a grin. "How did the luscious Max Williams respond to that? He doesn't look like someone who lets people tell him what to do."

"You forget, he's used to taking direction in his job."

"Only when he wants to, I'll bet."

An image of his dark, determined eyes rebelling against her suggestions the last time they worked together flashed into mind. "I think you're right."

"So, tell me everything," Carly demanded again.

"It was better than I expected." Well, that wouldn't have taken much. Now that the date was over, she should warn Carly about their mutual dislike. "As Tess mentioned, Max and I knew each other before. Remember when I did some freelance editing for the TV station? We met then. And later, we hired him to do some voiceover work at Lasting Productions. He acted like a naughty school boy, then I got all bossy and uptight about the schedule and the budget and all that." She bit her lip remembering some of their more unpleasant exchanges. "You know how I can get."

Carly nodded with a twinkle in her eye. "I know you're serious about your work, Anna, but it's not polite for me to point out how OCD you are about every little thing."

Annabel accepted the comment with a shrug and a grain of salt. "Too true."

"But weren't there *any* sparks? He is a hottie."

She scrunched her nose in distaste. "Yes, but he has kind of a wild reputation. You know, with women." She thought of her friend DeeDee and the questionable intern. And Candy LaBar, the stripper. And who knew how many others? Even rumors about Max and Tess Hartley had made the rounds when they were both new in town.

"I knew that." Carly waved the comment away. "That's why I picked him. I figured once you went out with a handful like Max, anyone that came along later would be a piece of cake."

"Why, you little stinker." Sometimes the girl showed more insight than the *Psychic Friends Network*. "And I was worried you'd be disappointed when you found out your attempt at matchmaking had missed its mark."

"Oh, well, I didn't expect you to fall madly in love and get married or anything, but going on *Let's Talk* announced to the single men in Cincinnati that you're available for a social life. Since you admitted the other night that you were ready to cut loose a little, I hoped I got it right, and that Max would be the perfect candidate. And you have another date coming up. Who knows? You might enjoy it."

Annabel stood up and began putting away the folded laundry. A hot mix of dread and excitement washed over her as she anticipated the possibility of another date with Max, but cold reality overshadowed both emotions. "Don't count on it, sweetie. I doubt that he'll pick up the second-date option."

While Max drank his first mug of coffee and caught up on the overnight news on CNN the next morning, he did his best to talk himself out of calling Annabel.

Confusing but tantalizing thoughts about her had kept him awake most of the night. The way the candlelight picked up about twenty different shades of blonde in her hair. The way her reserve disappeared with the first glass of champagne. The way her eyes glowed when she talked about her work. With each passing hour, he became more determined to peel away every one of her protective layers until he unleashed the passionate woman he'd glimpsed lurking beneath the touch-me-not exterior.

Bright morning light, however, revealed some serious drawbacks in the Get-To-Know-Annabel-Better Plan. Their rocky history, for one. Her snooty attitude, for another. The disdain she felt for his work, and her automatic assumption that anyone who liked to have a good time must be morally bankrupt, to name a few more.

To be fair, he remembered the times he'd goaded her with his worst behavior just to get a reaction from her.

Maybe it was crazy, but now that he thought about it, he wondered if she did the same thing with him in reverse.

Going back on his word and springing this bike trip on her as their second date seemed like asking for trouble. Especially if Mercer tried to make contact with him today as he'd promised.

But Max figured he'd take that chance.

The little weasel had failed to deliver the goods twice already. And the odds were high the informant would pull another no-show today. Max already had Roger standing-by to video the transaction if the deal actually went down. Recording the date with Annabel offered a good excuse for having him on hand.

Ready to make the call, he moved out onto his condo's balcony. The stunning view across the river usually helped clear his thoughts. With a freighter moving by beneath him, he flashed through the remaining negative arguments on his list.

She'd probably be a pain in the ass the whole day, and complain about the wind and the noise and the vibration.

Besides, they were in competition for a major award they both wanted and needed to win. She was bound to have hard feelings when she lost to him. Why spend more time with her than he had to?

Annabel embodied every attribute he avoided in a woman.

She made him think of home and hearth, needlepoint pillows and family barbecues on Sunday afternoons. And none of those things had anything to do with him.

He had his career and the freedom to do what he wanted. He had his family in Nashville, a few good friends, lots of fun-loving buddies, and plenty of fast, decorative women. He didn't need more than that.

The other kind of woman—Annabel's kind—took too much time, patience, and maintenance. In the end, the man's heart was smashed to pieces and his dreams lay in a pile of dust at his feet.

*No good.* That may have been his father's path, but it wasn't the route Max planned to take.

Instead of calling her, he went inside to plug his phone into the charger, then snatched up the television clicker to switch channels. Good, the top of the hour. Time for the next *SportsCenter.* He settled back to watch. But instead of following yesterday's baseball scores, his thoughts returned to Annabel.

He didn't like her. She didn't like him. They had nothing in common. Simple, right? Except for a couple of hours the night before, they had never done anything but rub each other the wrong way. But the memory of those few hours when the rubbing had been in all the right directions spurred his imagination.

His dick twitched at the thought of what she could do with that attention to detail of hers if she turned it on something besides work, duty, and strict adherence to the rules.

*What the hell?* He'd be doing the world a favor if he could get Miss Prim and Proper to loosen up a bit.

The feel of her head on his shoulder, the warmth of her breath on his neck, and the weight of her breast pressing against his arm at Music Hall had been hotter than the average lap dance. And when her hand had brushed his groin in the dark, he'd responded with as much enthusiasm as a kid sneaking a peek at his first centerfold. He'd been hornier than a toad ever since.

Max shook his head. Damn, this whole idea had disaster written all over it. He never put this much forethought into anything besides his work. But in the end, lust won out over common sense.

With his hand on his cell, ready to call her, his phone blew up with his father's ringtone, the first few bars of a George Strait song from the late eighties. It had been a family favorite ever since his dad had picked up a gig playing guitar on the recording when the regular Ace in the Hole picker needed an emergency appendectomy. Since Max's mom had left them earlier that same year, it provided his dad with a nice distraction. And the money from the studio session had helped, too.

"Hey, Dad."

"Hey, Max," he said in the rich twang that could switch from rockabilly to a country ballad in a single chord. "Got somebody who wants to talk to you."

"Male or female?" Max headed into the kitchen for another cup of coffee, needing possible fortification for the conversation ahead.

"We got ourselves a baseball situation here."

Male, then. Good. Baseball situations were easier for Max to deal with then a ballet or tea party drama from one of his nieces.

"Hey, Nath, what's up?" he asked after his dad passed off the phone to his oldest nephew. "Got a game today?"

"Yeah, Uncle Max." Six-year-old Nathan got right to the point. "My first real-pitch game. That's a lot harder than T-ball."

"It is harder, but more fun too. Just wait 'til the first time you nail the ball and that sucker goes sailing. There's nothing like it." Max smiled. Some of his best days had been spent on a ball field.

"But what if I strike out?"

Max knew not to laugh. His nephew took his baseball seriously. "Happens to the best of 'em."

"Did it happen to you?"

"More than half the time."

"Will the other kids laugh?"

"Not unless they're dumbasses." Damn, Ginger kept warning him not to cuss in front of the kids. They always ended up ratting him out, too, when she asked them where they picked up a particular term. "Don't tell your mother I said that. Tell her I called them, uh, buttheads."

"I'll tell her you said buttheads, but some of them *are* dumbasses."

Dumbasses abound, no matter what your age, he wanted to tell the boy, but settled on more acceptable advice. "Well, just watch the ball. If it's over your head, don't swing. If it's below

your knees, don't swing. When it's right for you, between belt-
and shoulder-high, swing like the devil. You'll make contact.
Trust me. And good luck. You and Grandpa should call me after
the game to let me know how it went."

"Will you come see me play?"

"Can't today, Slugger, but I'll get the schedule from your
mom and plan a date soon, okay? We'll work on your swing
then."

"Okay."

"Let me talk to Grandpa again."

"He's here."

"Good job, Max," his dad said when he took the phone
back. "He's been worried all week."

"Thanks, Dad," Max said, realizing he didn't say those
words often enough. "Thanks for everything." Thanks for
everything you did for me and the girls. Thanks for everything
you do for your grandchildren.

"Well, hey, whoa. That's unexpected, but gotta tell you,
raising you and your sisters, and now enjoying my grandchildren,
has brought me more pleasure than anything else in the world."

"More than music?"

"It wasn't like it was a choice. Children grow up. Music will
always be there. Music brings me joy and peace. It's part of my
soul, part of who I am. But you, Ginger, and Courtney are my
heart."

"What about our mother?"

A moment of silence separated them, then he heard his dad
sigh. "Son, I have to get this young'un to the ballpark. We can
have a philosophical discussion about life and love and women if
you want to, but do you want to have it right now? Is there
somethin' you're lookin' for exactly?"

Max scratched his head. He talked easily with his dad about
most things, but there were lines they usually didn't cross. Still
he dived into this one. "I wonder if you have regrets about
giving up your music career to take a sensible nine-to-five job
and help with homework instead."

"Best decision I ever made. When your mother left us, it
'bout broke my heart. Without the three of you, it'd still be
broke. You gave me three good reasons to get up every day and
to keep puttin' one foot in front of the other. And that's the
plain truth." His dad pulled the phone away from his mouth to

issue Nathan instructions about uniform, equipment, and water bottle. "Now, what's this about? Has a woman finally managed to tangle you up?"

"Nothing like that," Max said too quickly. "Just trying to make some career choices, wondering if you ever had regrets about yours."

"None you need worry about. Talk to you later." His dad chuckled. "And Max? Give the woman a chance, whoever she is."

If there were two things Max trusted, they were his dad and his gut. And both of them were telling him to give Annabel a call.

This time he didn't hesitate. He selected her number and waited as the phone rang. And rang.

On the verge of hanging up before Annabel's voicemail kicked in, a chirpy voice on the other end said, "Max?"

He recognized the teenybopper's youthful enthusiasm. "That's right, kiddo. Is Annabel around?"

"I knew it! I knew you'd call," Carly crowed. "Annabel didn't think you would, but when her phone rang, your name flashed on the screen. I had to answer it even though she hasn't been downstairs yet. I think she's still sleeping." She dropped her voice on the last word, as if sleeping late in their house was a secret. Or a crime. "Hang on. I'll take her the phone."

While he waited, he pictured Annabel draped across her bed, blond hair tousled, sheets in disarray. Remembering the red lace bra, he tried to imagine what unexpected thing she slept in. Probably something silky. Maybe something slinky. Definitely something sheer.

Or better yet, nothing at all.

He stifled a groan. For God's sake, he'd need another shower if she didn't hurry and pick up the damn phone.

"Max?" Her voice came over the line, sleep-warmed and husky. Wary... Sexy... Well worth the wait.

He had to clear his throat before he could speak. "I thought you'd be up already."

A noisy yawn answered him, followed by the rustle of covers being arranged and pillows being plumped. "Why?"

He liked keeping her off-balance. "Because I'll be over in about an hour."

"An hour?" she squeaked. "Why? What time is it now?"

"I have a proposition for you. Do you want to hear about it now or later?"

"Now, I guess."

"Remember last night when I said turnabout's fair play?"

"No."

"Sure you do," he prompted. "It was right before I kissed you. The first time. Not the second time, when we really got into it with tongues and hips and—"

"All right, already! I remember."

"Since I admitted I enjoyed myself on the boring date of your choice, I think we should go someplace of my choice today."

"Well, that's flattering," she said drily. "Why should I agree?"

"To prove to the television audience that you're as broad-minded and open to new experiences as I am."

"I don't have to prove anything."

"Of course you don't." He switched tactics. "But I also thought it would be a good comparison for us to make for Tess's show. You know, to see if we really are compatible."

"You know we're not."

"That doesn't mean we can't have some fun together while we broaden our horizons, does it? Come on," he cajoled. "Just this one time. Let the real Annabel come out and play."

Feeling her wavering, he forged ahead. "We're wastin' daylight, darlin'. Grab a bite to eat, drink plenty of liquids to get rid of whatever champagne hangover you've got and put on some clothes, if you feel obliged to. I'll be there shortly."

"Wait!" she said, and he did, expecting another argument. "What should I wear?"

*Gotcha.* "Black leather if you have any."

"Black leather?" She gulped. He actually heard her gulp. "As in whips and chains?"

A grin spread across his face at the note of panic in her voice. Sometimes having a bad reputation worked to his advantage. People expected the worst, and anything less made him look like an angel.

"Are you into that kinky stuff? I can change our plans if you want."

"No!" she croaked. "I mean, no." More throat clearing followed. "You're kidding, right? Of course, you're kidding. I'm sure whatever you have planned is fine. Um, Max?"

"Hmmm?"

"What exactly do you have planned?"

"Like last night, only one of us will know until we walk out your door. Deal?"

Silent seconds ticked by.

"Just one more question."

"Nope, this isn't *Jeopardy*. I'm all out of answers. You either want to go or you don't. Try to decide before I get there."

Annabel's eyes and temples pounded. Her teeth and cheeks hurt. Even her hair. Stomach, toes. Everything.

She downed two aspirin with her first cup of coffee, then tried to coax a slice of toast into settling easily on her queasy tummy. She'd like nothing more than to crawl back under the covers and coddle the first hangover of her life with the kid gloves it deserved. But she wouldn't put it past Max to come and pull her out of bed if she weren't ready and waiting when he arrived.

Taking her second cup of coffee out on the deck, she cleared her head with deep breaths of fresh spring air. A cheerful flat of pansies taunted her from the back steps. Gardening was one of the many chores that would remain undone today since she'd agreed to go somewhere with Max.

Somewhere with Max. *Yikes*. That sounded both ominous and thrilling.

Where? And why?

Why had he asked? And more importantly, why had she agreed?

Truth to tell, the butterflies fluttering around in her stomach were as much from anxiety as too much champagne. No telling what kind of activity Max considered *fun*. Probably something she considered immoral, illegal, or improper. Although it was hard to imagine anyone doing anything depraved on such a beautiful April morning.

She'd heard about Max's wicked reputation ever since he came to town. People at work said he led the pack at trying any hare-brained stunt at least twice. And when it came to women, apparently, he was the master of love 'em and leave 'em. Mindy, one of the besotted admins at work boasted that when he loved them, he left them smiling.

Of course, that wasn't always true.

Annabel had heard DeeDee crying and throwing up in the restroom a few weeks after Max glibly moved on to another victim. Poor deluded DeeDee defended Max instead of blaming him, but then she'd moved to Kansas before the baby arrived. Making a fresh start, in a new job, in a new city, with a new baby. DeeDee hadn't managed to keep in contact with Annabel beyond a few emails and texts. She got the feeling that DeeDee wanted to put Cincinnati and Max behind her.

In over her head, maybe Annabel should tell Max she wouldn't go with him today. Maybe she'd tell him she had to be back home by noon. Maybe she'd demand the truth from him about DeeDee. And the intern.

Right. And maybe she'd change her name to Angelina, marry Brad Pitt, and move to France.

She stretched out in the chaise, put her feet up, and closed her eyes. Searching for inner peace, she tried one of the relaxation techniques she'd learned during her husband's long illness. *Take strength from the ordinary pleasures of your surroundings, and* don't *think about fondling Max during Wagner's "The Ride of the Valkyries."*

Dang! Commanding herself not to think about it only made her think about it more.

Robins and larks twittered and fluttered around the bird feeder. A woodpecker tapped into an elm by the fence. Faint music drifted to her from a speaker in the kitchen. Children peddled tricycles on the driveway next to hers.

She pressed her fingertips to her temples as an engine roared nearby. Leave it to Mr. Malone next door to decide to get his yard work done early.

"Anna!" Carly called from inside. "Anna, come quick. You've *got* to see this."

Over the clambering objection of her headache, Annabel rushed through the house to the front porch. Carly stood on the sidewalk talking to one of her friends—a well-built guy wearing a helmet with a tinted face protector and straddling some monstrous-sized motorcycle.

The girl could just save her breath. No way would Annabel let her ride on that deathtrap.

She marched toward Carly just as the biker pulled off his helmet. The shock of discovering "Mad Max" in *Thunderdome* attire almost caused her to miss the bottom porch step.

"Come and see, Anna," Carly called out. "This is way better than a limo. Isn't it the coolest thing you've ever seen?"

Annabel remained near the house, leery of venturing any closer. "Oh, yes, the very coolest." Her voice and throat were as dry as dust.

The combination of gleaming black metal and chrome looked so alien, so dangerous, *and so masculine*. So suitable for Max, and so unsuitable for her. Maybe they could go wherever they were going in her car. Or she could follow him if he insisted on taking that hell-on-wheels machine.

"I *so* want to ride on this! Max says he'll take me for a spin."

"No!" Her screech jerked the evil little elves with trip hammers inside her head into motion again. Moderating her tone, she pressed her fingertips to her temples. "I mean, no. We probably don't have time for that, do we, Max?"

*Oh, my!* Focusing on Max for the first time, she took in the equally tantalizing and terrifying details of his appearance. This was the Max she'd heard about, the wild dare-devil—reckless and untamed, bold and exciting. What had happened to her semi-civilized, designer-suit-wearing escort from last night? The button-down shirt and tie had disguised the real Max—the one in black leather who scared her to death and set her pulse racing at the same time.

The jacket had two patches on the arm with diamond-shaped logos. One said Good Riders, the other said Awesome Good.

She pointed to the second one and lifted an eyebrow at him. "Bragging?"

"Nope, fact. I've got documentation if you want to see it." He opened a compartment on the back of the bike and tossed her a blue sports drink in a plastic bottle. "Here, drink this."

"Why?"

"Electrolytes. Good for a hangover."

"I had some coffee and toast, thank you." Barely suppressing a shudder, she moved to toss the bottle back to him.

He shook his head. "Rookie mistake. This is better. Drink it and go change."

She looked down at her clothes. "Why would I change?"

"You can't go like *that*." Dismissing her khaki pants, white T-shirt, and sandals with a flick of the wrist, he climbed off the bike and headed her way.

"Why not? You wouldn't tell me where we're going, but—"

"You'll be cold on the bike if you don't wear a jacket." He nudged her foot with the tip of a black leather boot. "And for safety's sake, the open-toed shoes have to go."

"Oh, right," she said with fake heartiness. "Like a pair of tennis shoes will be any protection when my body goes skidding across the pavement."

Her sarcasm provoked him into producing a heavy sigh. "That's not going to happen, but beginners always forget and put their feet down before the bike comes to a complete stop."

"You don't have to worry about me or my feet because I'm not going anywhere on that monstrosity."

"There's nothing to be afraid of, Anna," Carly encouraged. "I'll bet it's a lot like riding a roller coaster, isn't it, Max?"

He looked doubtful. "Do you like roller coasters, Morgan?"

"Not really."

He tilted his head to the side and considered her for a moment before shrugging and heading toward the bike. Regret pulled at her with each step that thudded against the concrete.

"After last night, I thought there might be more to you than meets the eye, but I guess I was right the other fifty times I met you." He settled himself on the seat and lifted his helmet from the handlebars. "Nice knowin' you, kid. See you around, Morgan."

"Wait!" Carly turned toward Annabel and actually stomped her foot, an action not seen from her since childhood. "Don't let him leave without you, Anna. You told me you were tired of living your life inside the safety of a familiar box. This is your chance to step outside it. At least, give it a try."

Old habits and fears kept Annabel mired in her own front yard. Carly faced Max again. "Will you take her up and down the street once, real slow, just so she can see what it's like?"

"Nah." He shook his head. "That'd be about as much fun as kissing my sister." He challenged Annabel with a lift of his eyebrow. "This isn't a moped, Morgan. When you go for a ride on a Harley, it should be a real ride, a *fast* ride, with nothin' half-assed about it. You've got to feel the noise to enjoy it."

He was taunting her. She *knew* he was taunting her and still the temptation shimmered before her eyes. If she had ever wanted to ride a motorcycle, this was probably the time. Besides, how fast could he go with Roger shadowing their every movement?

"Hey, wait a minute." Annabel's suspicions about Max started to ping on her internal safety radar again. "If this is the second date, where's Roger?"

"Since I didn't plan this in advance, I wasn't on his schedule. He'll catch up with us as soon as he can."

"Really." Skepticism oozed out of both syllables.

He shrugged a monumental shoulder. "I figured you'd prefer it this way. Do you want the world to see your fears and insecurities on Tess's show if this doesn't go well?"

"The authorities may need documentation on where to find my body," she muttered.

"Quit being a pain in the ass. You'll be fine." He checked the time on his phone. "Make up your mind."

Annabel took one pace, then a second one in his direction, before stopping. What would it be like to ride the wild beast for once instead of editing the fun through a viewfinder?

She looked at the motorcycle, so dark and shiny. She looked at Carly, so tense and eager. She looked at Max, so gorgeous and impatient. She looked at her life, so boring and dull. She sighed with disgust and impatience at the lackluster image. Just this once, she wanted desperately to go for it. What in the world was she waiting for?

"Don't leave!" She whirled toward the house. "I'll go change."

"Put on heavier pants and shoes—boots if you've got 'em and wear a jacket." He barked instructions from the sidewalk. "And don't forget the drink."

On the porch, she turned and gave a mock salute. "Yes, sir."

"Hey, it's for your own good."

"Or for my funeral."

His laughter floated to her as she mounted the stairs to her bedroom. Annabel pulled her hair free of its perennial bun. She gathered it into a low ponytail and bound it together with an elastic band. Considering how many pants and shirts she donned and discarded while trying to block the terror of venturing out on the first wild and unprotected ride of her life, she changed clothes in record time. Carly bounced in and vetoed her final choice of a yellow Polo shirt and v-neck sweater with Annabel's favorite black slacks.

"Biker chicks don't dress preppy," Carly teased.

"I am *not* a biker chick." Although the possibility sizzled through Annabel's imagination for one tantalizing moment.

"Not yet anyway." Carly ducked out of the room and returned with trendier items from her closet. "Try these."

After the switch, the only thing Annabel still wore that belonged to her was her underwear. Carly's clunky boots covered her feet from toe to ankle. A formfitting, midriff-skimming black knit shirt topped a pair of skinny black jeans that hugged her legs.

Annabel tugged and pulled the snug-fitting tee away from her midriff. "You don't think it's too, um, tight?"

"No, it's not." Carly left Anna's sensible poplin jacket on the bed and handed her a funky, studded denim one instead. "Don't worry. Wear this over it."

"I don't know." Annabel slid her arms through the sleeves and stared at herself in the mirror.

"It's not perfect," Carly said, "but it's the best we can do on short notice. Now, *go*, before he gets tired of waiting."

"Okay, okay." Annabel detoured to the bathroom. Before Carly shooed her down the stairs and out the door, she popped a couple more aspirin into her mouth and slugged them down with the blue wonder drink.

She returned to Max for inspection. Waiting for her on the porch, he looked up from texting and gave her a long assessing look. "Better" was his only comment. Tucking his phone into his jacket pocket, he encircled her small hand with his gigantic one and tugged her toward the bike. "Let's roll."

Carly trailed behind them. He handed Annabel a helmet, then took her purse, looked at it in disgust, and stuffed it in a saddlebag-thingy. She about ripped her ears off when she jammed the helmet onto her head, then fumbled fastening her chinstrap. It took her so long to adjust the only barrier she'd have between concrete and a cracked skull that Max finally tugged off a riding glove and stepped up to takeover.

Strong, capable hands snapped the strap into place before he flicked her nose with his finger. "All set. Hop on." He slid his glove back on.

She eyed man and machine with trepidation. "Any advice?"

"Relax," Carly suggested.

"Put your visor down or you'll get bugs in your teeth, and lean the same way I do on the curves," Max said. "Put these in." He dug into his pocket and held out a small plastic box.

"Earplugs?" She wrinkled her nose. "No, thanks." She'd prefer to hear the reassuring whoop-whoop-whoop of an emergency vehicle pulling up beside her if it came to that.

He shrugged then stuck the box back in his pocket. "Then, climb aboard and hang on."

Her heart thumped a mile a minute as she swung her leg over and perched behind him. She left as much room between them as possible—all of two inches if she measured right. "Hang on to what?"

"Me." With the devil's own grin, he took her hands and clasped them around his waist. His overwhelming presence smothered her, and she pulled back.

"Where are we going?" she asked, stalling.

"We're going on a day trip with my bike club."

"Oh, my." Her hand covered her heart as she pictured herself cowering in a gang of Hells Angels, while they drank whisky straight from the bottle, smoked dope, juggled switchblades, and compared tattoos of naked women.

"You got a problem with that?"

Maybe she *should* back out, after all. Now, while she was still on her home turf. Or maybe it wouldn't be as bad as she imagined. "Do you have a tattoo?"

"Sure. Want to see it?" His hands went to his belt buckle like he was ready to lower his jeans.

"No!" Swallowing hard, she leaned forward to whisper too low for Carly to hear. "Will there be nudity or drugs?"

"Not unless you want there to be, darlin'." He flipped her visor into place. That, combined with the growl of the engine, blocked her ears and drowned out his laughter.

And they were off.

# Chapter Four

Fear for life and limb replaced Annabel's lesser worries as Max revved the motor into a ferocious growl, shifted into gear, and sent them lunging forward with reckless speed. Between the noise and the motion, her poor head nearly exploded. The body rocking vibration of the black beast shook her insides like tapioca pudding.

She turned and looked with longing at her safe and solid house, as well as her beautiful, lively daughter waving them on their way. Annabel wanted to wave back, one final farewell, but her hands refused to unclench from their death grip on Max's jacket.

When they turned a corner and the house disappeared from sight, she closed her eyes and buried her forehead against the wall of black leather in front of her. The relentless rumble of the engine filled her ears and echoed around inside her helmet, accompanied by a tremor that rattled her brain and pounded against her eardrums.

During what seemed like an eternity, she took a quick inventory of her life and her unfulfilled goals. She really should have tried to patch things up with her sister. She'd never have the chance to study with cinematographer Lance Foreman as she'd always wanted to do. And the dream of living and working in New York or LA would remain just that—a dream, not a reality, or even a possibility. Suddenly, it seemed like an unendurable loss that she'd never *seen* Paris, France. Or Versailles, France. Or even Versailles, Indiana, for that matter.

And wouldn't it be a travesty to win the Community First award posthumously?

At the very first stop, she should call Carly and tell her she loved her...and remind her where to find the key to the safety deposit box.

Just as Annabel decided they must be near Columbus by now, the bike decelerated and the vibration decreased. She ventured a peek to see if she recognized her surroundings.

And she did.

They idled at a traffic light not a mile from her house.

"Stop." She tapped Max on the shoulder, and he turned his head to look at her. "Stop," she shouted, motioning for him to pull into a filling station on the corner.

With a twist of his wrist and an energetic vroom, he obeyed. While they rolled to a stop, she put her feet down, scuffing the toes of Carly's boots and almost ripping her feet from her ankles. She slammed into him with an *ooph*! and scrambled to regain some distance between her chest and his back. Okay, she admitted grudgingly, so sometimes he was right.

He cut off the motor. "What's wrong?" His voice sounded distant and sinister behind his dark face mask. Like Darth Vader without the cape.

Her hands shook as she lifted her Plexiglas face covering. Breathing deeply, she savored a moment of peace and quiet and immobility. "How fast were we going?"

"Only about seventy," he drawled. "I can't really crank it up until we're on the highway."

"Seventy!" Annabel jumped off the bike onto solid ground. "That's reckless and dangerous! Give me my purse and I'll walk home from here."

He lifted his shield and she could see his grin. "You're so easy to rile, Morgan. I stayed within the speed limit the whole time, which on this street is thirty. Now, get back on, or we'll be late."

"Oh, sor-ry." Hiding her deep-down feeling of foolishness behind sarcasm, she accepted his hand and climbed back on. "I didn't realize the Hells Angels were such rigorous schedule-keepers."

He shrugged. "You know how it is. Villages to pillage, towns to plunder." At least, this time she recognized his lame attempt at humor. He pulled her arms around him, then joined her hands together in front of him. Holding them in place, he turned to look at her. "Try to keep an open mind," he suggested. "You don't know half as much as you think you do."

*Wasn't that the truth?* She'd been raised to live a respectable, responsible life of suffocating decorum. Her job as a documentary editor suited her perfectly, isolating her in safety while she observed and edited the reckless activities of others. From a safe distance, she could decide what footage could be kept and what could be cut.

She'd hardly experienced anything firsthand, and she knew without asking that firsthand was the way Max experienced everything. Determined to do this for herself, for her stepdaughter, and to show Max a more interesting side of her, she'd try living life his way for just one day. She nodded for him to take off. Following his advice, she kept her eyes wide open and her head up.

The scenery flew by in a blur. Colors and shapes zipped past in a flowing kaleidoscope. Gradually, her body and her vision adjusted to the unaccustomed motion and velocity. The sensation of freedom and daring, of racing the world and winning, reminded her of the champagne from the night before, fizzy and fun and going straight to her head.

At least she enjoyed it until they passed from the structured residential streets onto the terrifying rush of I-275. SUVs and minivans the size of tanks sped past them and brushed close beside them. Annabel's vulnerability increased, and she cowered behind Max—the only stable object in an unsteady universe.

Pressing her chest against the strong column of his back, she clasped her arms in a bear hug around his middle and wedged his hips between the V of her thighs. Somehow the idea of fusing herself to his comforting bulk provided her with a feeling of safety.

An eighteen-wheeler barreled alongside and spewed exhaust and gravel in their direction while sucking the air around them like a giant vacuum cleaner. Too bad her clothing choices hadn't included something more practical for motorcycle riding than faded denim—like a suit of armor.

Just before she lost all control and succumbed to screaming hysterics, Max took the Ellis Road exit toward Riverbend Music Center and the Ohio River. Off the highway, the air blasting past her became fresher, cleaner, and lighter. After a couple more turns off of smooth pavement onto bumpy byroads, lush green countryside enveloped them in a simpler world. One filled with nothing more than dappled sunlight, a powerful engine, and an incredibly sexy man creating a decided hum of awareness between her thighs.

Raising her head, Annabel relished the unforeseen pleasure of traveling unencumbered through time and space. Why had she resisted? She'd been wrong, and she would admit it when they stopped. If they ever stopped. And she wasn't sure she wanted to. At least not while she had this little sensual buzz building. Feel the noise, indeed.

Before the buzz took her where she wanted to go, the Harley began to slow. She leaned into another turn, and the gravel road ratcheted her sexual pleasure up a notch. But looking up ahead, she couldn't believe her eyes. Through her near orgasmic gaze, she blinked and looked again.

Under a banner that read "Good Riders - Ride a Bike, Feed a Tyke," Harleys, Harleys, and more Harleys filled the parking lot of The Hog Heaven Bar and Grill. Each machine carried a biker more disreputable looking than the next. She wondered at the number of cows killed to produce so much black leather. When Max said they were meeting his bike club, she'd pictured a gang of ten or twenty, not a legion.

As they reached the fringe of the group, men gestured and called out greetings to Max. As he had predicted, Annabel couldn't hear a thing, but he nodded and waved. Slowing the bike to a crawl, he threaded it through the gathering.

At the bar's rambling porch, he pulled into an empty space. A tall, wiry-looking guy in chaps, plaid shirt and leather vest leaned against a beam. Despite world-weary eyes and lines on his face that told of a life lived hard, he carried an undeniable aura of authority. A blue bandana covered most of his red hair peppered with gray. In the goatee he stroked, the gray strands outnumbered the red. He waited for Max to shut off his bike. Annabel wanted to whimper when the engine finally quit pulsating.

"Glad you could make it," Goatee Man said to Max.

Or so Annabel guessed. With the residual ringing in her ears, she had to rely on lip-reading more than hearing.

The man handed an envelope to Max. He stuck it in the back pocket of his jeans, millimeters away from grazing Annabel's most personal place with those long-ranging fingers. The thought should be horrifying, instead of making her dizzy with longing.

She couldn't make out Max's response to Goatee Man's conversation, but from the other guy's grin and nod in her direction, that was just as well. If she looked as ready to come as she felt, she didn't want to know.

Max swiveled at the waist to face her. His mouth moved,

but the words jumbled together.

Annabel took off her helmet and cupped her ear. "What?"

"We'll only be here a few minutes." He mouthed each word distinctly and pointed to his watch. "You need to take care of anything?"

*Him.* She wanted to take care of him. Or have him take care of her. Insane, but it was all she could do to keep from grabbing him. She needed to get a grip before she attacked the man and stripped him naked. But maybe he wouldn't mind. The idea of a naked Max should scare the bejesus out of her. But instead, she found the idea... intriguing as all get out. Something she'd have to think about at greater length. Sometime when he wasn't standing right in front of her in all his audacious glory.

He'd told her there wouldn't be drugs or nudity unless she wanted there to be, and maybe, just maybe, she did. Not drugs, of course, but nudity sounded awfully appealing.

Annabel shook her head. No, it didn't. Not really. All of this jittery sensation was simply a reaction to the crotch rocket she'd been riding, the sexy body of the man she'd had her thighs wrapped around, and years of sleeping alone. She didn't even like Max, and all that sexy allure he exuded was definitely off-limits. But that didn't prevent him from looking damned good to a libido that was giddy from a long overdue dose of shake, rattle, and roll.

Annabel eyed the seedy-looking dive and the crowd of mostly men. No one she eyeballed looked half as good—or even as reputable—as Max. Better to stick with the devil she knew.

Her legs trembled so much, she wasn't sure she could stand. Her jaws along with every other molecule of her body still quivered from the ride, and she didn't trust herself to speak. She shook her head at Max and signaled her intention to stay put.

After more mumbled conversation, Goatee Man climbed aboard an enormous bike. Then the army of road warriors thundered their Harleys into a ground-trembling roar, equaling the decibel level of a NASA liftoff.

Lines and rows formed like magic from the random scattering of riders. Two bikers pulled into the road, blocking the approaching traffic as the platoon of motorcycles fell in behind Max and the man with the goatee, leading them on a journey Annabel knew not where.

Wherever they were going, they were going full force, and

they weren't keeping a low profile. And she hoped it took them a long time to get there.

From the way Annabel molded herself to his back like hot wax, Max expected more questions or complaints when he pulled into the next stop. Instead, she swung her leg over the bike like a veteran rider, even though her limbs appeared as wobbly as Gumby's. Instead of complaining, she merely rested her rump against the seat and lifted off her brain bucket emitting a low, vibrating hum.

Somewhere along the way, she'd lost the hard edges that usually kept her face pulled taut. She looked softer and sweeter and wore a dreamy, self-satisfied smile he'd never seen on her lips before. If he knew anything about women, he'd think she…

Well, son-of-a-bitch! She'd gotten revved up enough to experience her own personal moment of glory! And he hadn't even gotten to participate with so much as a finger in the process. She'd felt the noise, all right. If he'd known she was that ripe and ready, he'd have played this trip differently from the start.

"You need to freshen up?" he asked, halfway hard just thinking of her climaxing while pressing against his back.

He fought an urge to touch the new and pliable Annabel. Hell, he fought the urge to kiss her, touch her, imprint himself all over her while she swam in the sensual pool of afterglow. When she remembered coming apart in satisfaction, he wanted her to connect him to those happy memories. He'd made them possible, after all, even if he hadn't been personally involved.

That sure wouldn't be the case next time.

She pounded the heel of her hand against her ear. He recognized the sure-sign for temporary Harley deafness. Harleys weren't known for being smooth, sleek, or dependable, but they over-compensated for all that by being loud, fast, and sexy. No point in trying to talk to her now. Her ears would ring for a while.

Putting his hand on her wrist, he stroked his thumb across her pulse. When her lips turned up in a small smile of awareness, he pointed her toward the bar and mimed eating and drinking.

Annabel looked askance at the dilapidated exterior of a honky-tonk the club frequented called The Hoghouse. Clearly, it didn't meet her prissy-girl standards, even though her prissy-girl standards had tumbled a notch or two in the last half hour.

With a hand on her shoulder, he motioned for her to wait while he went inside to do the glad-handing bit he'd missed out on earlier. There, the other Hog-lovers bought smokes or Cokes and waited in line to get the next card for their poker hand. Each rider hoped to have the winning combination at the end of the run. But Max's thoughts kept returning to Annabel getting herself off on his bike.

"Thanks again for coming today," Dick Ubecki, the club president, said to him. "We always get a good turnout when the fellas know you're coming along, and this one's for a good cause."

"Happy to help out, Judge," Max said. "How many riders do we have?"

"A couple hundred."

Max nodded. That many entry fees would make a hefty donation to the Feed-a-Child Foundation. "It's a great day for a ride."

"Any day's a great day for a ride." Bruce Townsend joined them with a root beer in hand. "Especially if you're a Good Rider."

Max and Dick slapped palms with Bruce, a tubby physician who looked more like the Pillsbury Doughboy's version of Ozzie Osborne than a respected member of the AMA.

"What is it with you doctors and Harleys, Bruno?" Dick asked. "There are probably more of you here than there are at the hospital."

Bruce shrugged. "Riding's a hell of a stress-reliever."

"And you guys are about the only ones who can afford the price of an upscale bike these days," Dick cracked.

"Looks like you judges do all right," Bruce said. "When did you trade up for that V-Rod?"

"Last month. You should feel the way she handles—slicker than a swimsuit model's well-oiled skin."

Max tuned out the conversation, checking to see if the line at the bar had cleared out enough for him to get his poker card. He didn't like leaving Annabel alone for long in the middle of this group of mostly horny, middle-aged wannabe players.

Tim Addams, Max's financial advisor, crossed the room and clapped him on the shoulder. Tim handed over a white envelope with a card inside. "Picked this up for you."

Damn, he'd forgotten Tim would be here. He wasn't a wannabe player. He was the Ultimate Player. Max had known him to sample more women in a week than most men had meals. That was a good week, even for Tim, but still.

Now more eager than ever to get back to Annabel, Max stuck the envelope into his back pocket and headed for the door. "Thanks. Maybe I'll get lucky today." From this angle, he watched Annabel bend toward the rearview mirror while she pulled a comb through honey-colored curls.

"Looks like you already have." Tim nodded toward Annabel and the excellent view of her truly gorgeous ass. "Who's the lady? She looks more like my type than yours."

Max frowned and considered his friend. He was a good guy to have on hand at the poker table, to make the rounds with on the golf course, or in the clubs on a night out. Tim looked like an overgrown choirboy with the muscular build of Beckham and the personality of a snake charmer. For some reason, that combination appealed to a lot of women who ended up either sleeping with Tim or investing great sums of money with him. Or both.

Max invested great sums of money with him, too, but only because the snake charmer was a financial genius. And normally, Max didn't care how many women Tim screwed. There were more than enough women out there to go around. But Max balked at the idea of Tim turning his dubious charms Annabel's way. The guy did have an eye for selecting quality women. Max would give him that. "How can you tell from here?"

"She doesn't have on Spandex or glitter."

Max smirked. He knew something Tim didn't. She'd worn red lace the night before, and if there was a God, she'd have on something equally sexy today. "Maybe she does underneath."

"I don't think so." Tim shook his head, not buying the bluff. "So why's she with you?"

"I dared her to come."

Tim laughed and nudged Max with his elbow. "Introduce me and I'll take her off your hands."

Max shrugged off the suggestion. "She's no trouble." *Not at the moment anyway.* "Maybe later. We're about ready to head out." He left Tim to rejoin Annabel, watching as she flipped her gleaming hair off her shoulder with a beguiling head toss.

"How're you doing?"

She flashed a dazzling smile. The sun bounced off the various shades of blonde in her hair, begging him to run his fingers through it. Pretty. And more intriguing still, sexy. He tried to remember if he'd ever seen it unleashed before. Not that he could recall. The effect made her look younger, more approachable. Of course, the recent orgasm could have brought on that look, too.

Annabel cupped her ear and hollered, "What?"

Damn, he'd forgotten her temporary hearing loss. Leaning closer, he repeated the question, getting a heady whiff of lemony shampoo as he did so.

"Brushing out my hair," she said, loud enough for people across the river to hear.

"Not '*what* are you doing'." He pushed a lock of silky hair behind her ear. "*How?*"

"'Now' what?"

"Never mind." Chuckling, he reached into his pocket to pull out the earplugs again. "Ready for these?"

She nodded as she smoothed her hair back with her hands and tried to slip an elastic band around it.

He took her hand in his, plucked the elastic from her fingers, and placed the earplugs in her palm. "Trade you."

"Hey, I need that."

He shook his head. "I like it down." She couldn't hear him, but flushed, and he imagined she got the gist. She smiled, nodded, and slipped the earplugs in. He could do with a whole lot more of this agreeable attitude than the contrary approach she usually took.

And this time, she hopped into place behind him like a pro. With a hand signal from Dick, the two-hundred engines revved into life. Annabel's thighs aligned with Max's and her arms circled him as they led the herd of riders onto the road.

She felt more relaxed against him than she had at first, but then, so would a goalpost. She also seemed to get the hang of leaning with the bike instead of away from it, and her feet quit stomping on her imaginary brakes. Of course, his jacket might have her fingerprints imprinted on it for life, but he could live with that.

This next section of smooth road probably wouldn't escalate into the kind of release she'd already experienced, but he'd just as soon she didn't loosen up too much. A lot of daylight stretched ahead of them. If she managed to stick it out, he wanted to keep her close and slightly jazzed. A tandem ride on a bike provided the perfect opportunity for Annabel to become acquainted with the feel of his body against hers.

For a couple of disappointing minutes back at her house, he'd thought he'd end up leaving her behind. But aside from managing to get herself off and being a little shell-shocked, so far, she'd hung in there.

Her legs tightened around him again as they reached a small suspension bridge. He and Dick had led the group all the way across before he realized the cell phone in his shirt pocket vibrated. With one hand, he pulled it out and checked the number.

Mercer.

He'd have to find a way to ditch Annabel for a bit and contact the snitch at the next stop.

"We'll be here for a half an hour." Max enunciated the words carefully after Annabel removed her earplugs. "What would you like for lunch?"

And even though she could now make out some, if not all, of the conversation around her, she appreciated having a good reason to focus on his mouth.

He steered her toward a picnic table on the patio of yet another sketchy dive, the Blue Moon Saloon. She'd never realized there were so many out-of-the-way spots in the midst of Southwest Ohio tailor-made for eating, drinking and getting into who knew how many kinds of trouble. She definitely needed to get out more. Not to these kinds of places, necessarily, but at least to expand her horizons. Or ask Max to expand them for her.

Without his hand to keep her grounded, the phantom vibration of the bike rattled her body like a mini-earthquake. Exhaling a small sigh, Annabel sank onto the solid support of a wooden bench.

"Cae— Cae—" She stopped to clear the pound of road grit from her throat before choking out her request. "Caesar salad with grilled chicken and iced tea."

Max rolled his eyes. "You don't want salad. This is the Blue Moon, darlin'. They're famous for barbecue, barbecue, or barbecue. Those are the choices." He'd ticked all three of them off on his fingers. "They might have potato salad or coleslaw, but trust me, Caesar salad is not on the menu."

"Do they have barbecue chicken?"

"Mouth-watering." His smile matched the description.

"Great, I'll take mine plain, please."

"Without sauce?" he asked, clearly aghast. "That's about as exciting as having sex without a partner." Shaking his head, he went off to get their meals.

After her amazing experience on the back of his bike, she might have disputed that comment. She clapped a hand over her mouth to keep a surprised spurt of laughter from escaping.

Although she hadn't been with anyone since Carl, her dear but unexciting husband had been polite and methodical in bed, sad to say. Since his death, she'd kept a vibrator hidden on the top shelf of her closet behind a box of old photographs. It seemed like a Barbie toy compared to the adult-sized pulsation created by the machine of steel she'd been riding this morning. *So size does matter.*

Max couldn't really know what had happened to her back there on that bumpy stretch of road, could he? She'd done her best to contain her reaction by squeezing her thighs tightly, pressing her forehead into his back and clenching her hands in front of him—against his rock hard abs, actually. But he did have that reputation for reading women, so maybe he'd noticed the subtle signs.

While she waited for his return, she concentrated on relaxing her sore and tense muscles. It would take more than the half-hour allotted for lunch for her thighs to unclench. Even though she was almost a puddle in some areas, other body parts were still clenched tighter than a corset.

A little embarrassed over her earlier *response*, Annabel was grateful that they'd been following a road that had more potholes than pavement for most of the morning. Whatever the road lacked in smoothness, its route alongside the Ohio River more than made up for in scenic beauty.

From her perch on the bench, Annabel noticed that the Blue Moon's patio overlooked the river's swelling banks. A large limb bobbed in and out of the water. A flock of geese honked overhead. A canopy of branches blocked the sun with a haze of bright green leaves bursting to life. The idyllic setting couldn't keep her thoughts from drifting to the puzzling white envelopes she'd seen members of the group surreptitiously peeking into before pocketing.

What did they contain? Something as harmless as the location of the next stop or something dangerous like one of the new synthetic drugs she'd heard was spreading through Cincinnati like an epidemic? She'd ask Max about the envelopes at the first opportunity. But if they contained something top-secret or illegal would he tell her the truth?

Keeping an eye on the driftwood's progress, she became aware of two guys talking on the other side of the plank fence behind her.

"I checked with my dealer yesterday, and he can't keep up with my demands anymore. Have you had any trouble, Bruno?" a rumbling baritone asked.

"Not since I switched suppliers," a tenor responded. "Who've you been using?"

"Royce out of Tallahassee."

"Yeah, I heard some untimely press about illegal aliens brought them some unwanted attention from several federal agencies. It slowed down their operation so much that distribution isn't making it much north of Tennessee."

"I don't want trouble with the Feds," Baritone grumbled. "I don't need those snoops poking around more than they do already."

"Who does?" Tenor asked. "Call me later, and I'll hook you up with my supplier. He might be able to get his hands on what you need."

"At what price? And how soon?"

"It'll be expensive, but it beats not being able to meet the demand."

"I don't have much choice. I need those drugs. Some of my people are desperate enough to pay any amount."

Covering her mouth to hold back her gasp, Annabel leaned back to catch a glimpse of the conspirators. She might need to pick them out of a lineup at some point. One was chubby with a long ponytail. The other one was ferret-like, slim and edgy, sporting a gold hoop earring and a skull-and-crossbones do-rag.

As they moved out of earshot, Annabel considered what to

do with the information she'd overheard. She'd learned enough at the high school filming *Challenging Destiny* to know that not all drug dealers lurked in back alleys and looked like gang-bangers or street thugs.

Her initial reaction was to go off half-cocked, but she kept herself in check. If she panicked, she'd call attention to herself. Probably a bad choice. She could leave and forget all about her suspicions. Or call the police with an anonymous tip. Probably the choice the old, more boring Annabel would make.

Or she could play it cool and try to discover the drug dealers' identities before she called her vice-cop neighbor and have him bring in reinforcements. Since she wasn't in any immediate danger, she liked the last choice the best. This could be the start of a new career. Investigative journalism. True crime documentaries. Breaking news stories.

Hah! If he weren't careful, she'd give Max a run for his money in areas besides the Community First award.

Just then the leader of the bikers—Goatee Man—and another biker guy dropped into seats across from her and set their platters of ribs on the table. A younger leather-clad guy slid himself and a couple of pulled pork sandwiches into the space to her left.

"Mind if we join you?" Goatee Man asked, somewhat after the fact. "Where's Max? I didn't notice him inside."

"He was on his cell, talking to his nephew. He'll be along soon," the one beside Goatee Man said, switching his attention to Annabel. "I wanted him to introduce us, but since he's not here, I'll take care of it myself. I'm Tim, and this is Dick, our fearless leader." He pointed to the third man. "That's Gabe. We're all friends of Max's."

"Hi, I'm Annabel." As she shook hands with Tim, he held onto hers a fraction longer than necessary. But when she looked up at him to see if he meant anything by it, she couldn't resist returning his smile. He looked more clean-cut than the others and was kind of cute in an Opie-Taylor-meets-Metallica sort of way. Gabe, the third guy in the trio, was handsome, quiet, even a little reserved, but just as confident and self-assured as the other two.

Tim studied her openly. "What's a nice girl like you doing here with a guy like Max?"

"Why wouldn't I be here with Max?" She'd gradually

figured out that Max was a lot less harmful than she'd thought. But after overhearing the drug dealers and noticing the white envelopes sticking out of random pockets, Tim's comment made her wonder all over again. Of course, if she judged others by the company they kept, these three guys wouldn't be above reproach—and neither would she. There were always two sides to every story. As a filmmaker, she prided herself on remembering that.

"He's never brought a date on a ride before," Gabe said.

"Most of the women he knows don't roll out of bed before noon," Tim contributed, ruining Gabe's attempt at diplomacy.

"A lot of news people work late hours." Annabel refused to rise to the bait. Strippers kept late hours, too, but the last thing she wanted was to hear about Max's female companions or to be lumped in with them. "Besides, this might not qualify as a date."

"What is it?" The curiosity in Tim's eyes heated up as he squirted an extra dose of sauce on his rack of ribs.

"We were set-up as a matchmaking thing on *Let's Talk*, and he kind of dared me to come with him today."

Tim grinned, revealing a small Opie-like gap between his two front teeth. "That's what he said."

"Didn't you believe him?" she asked.

"We-ell, sometimes, the truth-according-to-Max bears little resemblance to the real thing. Especially where women are concerned." Tim's words seemed to contain a warning she didn't need.

As stunningly attractive as Max Williams was, he was not her type. But he could be fun and exciting, and that was all she needed for today.

"No resemblance to what?" Max set a plate of plain grilled chicken and coleslaw in front of her. He deposited his own loaded plate in the small, empty space to her right.

"The truth," Tim said.

"You can't be talking about me," Max objected. "I'm almost Clark Kent, a mild-mannered reporter in search of truth, justice, and the American way."

Forking into her chicken, she realized that he took his promotional slogan as "The People's Reporter" more seriously than his self-mocking implied.

"Always around when there's trouble," Gabe ribbed.

"Leading poor Lois into trouble, too," Tim jabbed.

Annabel blinked as all three of Max's friends looked her way. "I'm not poor anybody, and no one has ever tried to lead me into trouble." Now, why did that statement sound more like a complaint than a recommendation?

"I didn't think they had," Tim said with a wink. "Plus, you're miles out of Max's league." He tipped his can of soda in her direction in a silent salute.

"Thank you, I think." Rather than accustom herself to the spine-tingling thrill of Max's thigh pressed against hers, she tried to ease away from him. When he quickly closed the gap, she gave up the retreat. It seemed silly to avoid such innocent contact after they'd been touching a lot more than thighs all morning.

"No, she's not. We're in the same league." Max looked up from removing the onion from his sandwich. "We're nominated in the same category for the Community First award."

"Nice," Dick offered. "Congratulations. I like an accomplished woman."

"Way to go, Annabel," Tim said. "Which entry is yours?"

"It's called *Challenging Destiny*." Her cheeks glowed with pride. Bless Max for bringing up the subject.

"Hey, I saw that one," Gabe said. "They showed it at P&G the other day as part of the United Way's pitch for corporate sponsors. Great piece of work." He answered her smile with one of his own. "What did you do on the project? Write? Produce? Direct?"

"All of the above," she said. "My title was associate producer, but it was a four-year labor of love, and I ended up holding just about every job description." She remembered the fulfilling hours with satisfaction.

"So you're a producer?" This from Tim.

"I wish. We were very low budget, and I came cheap when the original producer moved on to another project." She held up her crossed fingers. "If I win the award maybe I'll get a promotion and the title, but with a daughter on her way to college, I'm just happy to be employed."

"You're not old enough to have a daughter on her way to college," Dick objected.

"Stepdaughter," Annabel explained.

"You're married?" Tim asked.

"Widowed," Annabel told him.

"Ah. That explains a lot." Tim nodded wisely before adding an "ooph" when Dick's elbow connected with his ribs.

Gabe cleared his throat. "When's the award ceremony?"

"Next Friday."

"Are you taking Shawntel?" Dick asked Max.

*Shawntel?* Annabel frowned. The name sounded like it belonged to another stripper. Didn't the man know anyone named Jennifer or Sally?

"She's not sure she can go."

"She *should* go," Dick insisted. "If it hadn't been for her, you wouldn't have done that piece—"

"She hasn't decided yet, Dick." Max's comment cut off his friend. When Dick raised questioning eyebrows at Max, Annabel saw him slant his eyes in her direction.

"Oh, right. Well." Dick stood up. "Think I'll go get a piece of that cherry pie before we head out. Anybody want anything?"

"No thanks." Max checked his watch. "Annabel?"

"None for me, thanks."

Tim turned a high-voltage smile her way. "If Dick's still feeding his face, that means we have time to stretch our legs, Annabel. How does a stroll by the river sound before getting back on Max's monster hog?"

# Chapter Five

"Well, um... maybe a very short one." Placing her palms on the table, Annabel prepared to push herself to her feet. Max's friend had been so nice, refusing would seem rude. But she worried her rubbery legs would collapse beneath her. With Max, Dick, Tim, and Gabe watching, she hoped she wouldn't fall on her face.

"I guess you've already got somebody taking care of your bike." Max made the statement as he slid his arm around Annabel's waist, holding her in place.

"My bike?" Tim's eyes widened. "No, why?"

"The rear tire looked a little low when we pulled in. I thought you knew."

"No! I didn't. Annabel, excuse me! See you at the next stop." Tim reached the bottom of the patio steps before the last word floated back to her.

While he polished off a rib, Gabe looked at Max accusingly. "I saw what you did there. There's nothing wrong with Tim's tire."

"There might be."

"That was mean." Annabel didn't try to hide her smile.

"From your expression, I didn't think you wanted to go for a walk." He wiped his mouth and fingers with a napkin. "But I'll get him if you'd like."

She held up a restraining hand. "No, thanks. Maybe I'll just rest a while longer."

He narrowed his eyes and studied her. "How're you really holding up? Pretty sore?"

"I'm good." She smiled brightly so he wouldn't guess the truth and offer to let her skip the rest of the ride. Going home now didn't seem nearly as appealing as it had before. An idea had been germinating in her brain about a documentary on a biker club, with or without a drug angle. The visuals would be spectacular.

Maybe she should run the idea by Max first. Maybe bike

clubs didn't like a lot of publicity. Or he could be here investigating a breaking story himself. "I'm really enjoying myself, but—"

A woman dressed in Harley-logo overkill slid onto the other bench. "This your first road trip, honey? You wouldn't like it nearly so well if you had to ride at the tail end of the group and eat dust and fumes all day long."

"I was wondering about that. How do Max and I rate riding in front?"

"You're with our local celebrity," Gabe said. "When Max rides with us, he gets front and center. We like to show him off."

"Oh, shut up and eat," Max said without any real heat, "or else we'll be here all day." He checked the time again. "And I'd like to get to the final destination before nightfall."

"Fifteen more minutes," Dick said, returning with a piece of pie. "Then we ride. Go spread the word. And remind 'em to see the dealer."

"Right." Max stood and pulled Annabel up with him. His strong hand under her arm held her steady until she had her feet firmly planted. He continued to hold on as she stepped over the bench. She expected him to let go of her then, but he tucked her arm through his and pulled her close. "Come on, Annabel. If you don't want to walk, I know a nice place for you to wait."

All too aware of his solid body next to hers, she worked hard to keep a casual tone. "Um, yeah, sure. I keep meaning to ask you—"

"Hey, Max, have you seen Gordo's new bike?"

"Hey, Max, you going on the ride to Minnesota next month?"

"Mad Max, know anybody interested in a deal on a Fat Boy?"

Every few steps someone high-fived him or called for his attention. Without seeming to slight anyone, he kept on moving until he pulled her around the side of the building. They stopped beside an old-fashioned swing hanging from a huge oak tree.

"Have a seat." He made an exaggerated sweeping gesture.

She looked at the sturdy rope-and-board contraption for several seconds before circling it in amazement. "I don't even remember the last time I sat on one of these." Breaking into a wide smile, she almost clapped her hands in delight.

"It's easier than riding a bicycle. You never forget how."

Max steadied the ropes while she lowered herself into place. "Didn't you ever take Carly to the playground? Or let someone push you during a picnic?"

"Carly was past the playground stage when I married her father." And Carl would have thought it beneath a professor's dignity to do something so frivolous. Marriage to an older man had stifled spontaneity. The compensations had included companionship, stability, security, and Carly, of course.

Annabel sat for a few seconds, pushing herself back and forth with her feet firmly planted.

"What about boyfriends in elementary school, high school, or college?"

Lifting her feet, she leaned her shoulders forward and then back to generate a bit of motion. "Oh, there weren't many of those."

With silence stretching between them, she wished she'd cut out her tongue before admitting that pathetically sad fact to a man who went through women like peanuts at a ballgame.

After a moment, she glanced over her shoulder at Max. Before she could decide if the odd expression on his face was pity or disbelief, he set his hands next to her hips on the wooden seat and pulled it back, before giving her a strong push forward.

She raised her feet, beginning the pumping action required to keep going. On the backward arc, Max pushed again. Up and back, she soared higher and higher. The gentle breeze flowed through her hair beneath the awning of branches and leaves, making her feel airy and free.

She owed this feeling to Max, this lightening of spirit. Carefree, she stretched her legs and reached for the sky with her toes. She turned to throw him a smile over her shoulder. All her worries and responsibilities slid right off her shoulders and straight to the ground.

Her body immediately followed.

The rough rope scuffed her palms and tore at the flesh before she flailed through the air with the grace of an elephant. Hurtling toward terra firma, she closed her eyes and prepared for immediate and immense pain. Out of nowhere, she hit a solid brick wall. With arms.

Somehow Max managed to pluck her from mid-air. He stumbled, caught himself, then stumbled again, toppling them both to the grass.

Cradled in his arms, Annabel landed spread eagle on top of him. The world teetered and tottered as she lifted her whirling head. When the stars, birds, and fireworks finally settled down, she found herself splayed against him. She levered herself up and stared straight into his glittering eyes. "I guess I was supposed to hold on."

He clasped her tightly to him with one hand and smoothed along the lines of her body with the other. Searching for broken bones, no doubt. "You all right?"

Flustered by the intimacy and a surge of desire, she gulped and nodded before stopping his roaming hand in mid-roam.

He grinned and folded his hands behind his head as if lounging at the beach. "Nice dismount. I'd give it a ten."

Behind the grin, his dark eyes studied her. Every inch of his body hardened beneath hers. A pulse beat rapidly at the hollow of his throat.

Was it only the years of sexual deprivation that made her want desperately to press her lips against that pulse and lick up to his jaw, feeling the rough stubble where his beard shadowed his skin? Or was it the thrill of danger, the delicious appeal of the bad boy, the attraction of the unknown that beckoned to the recklessness she'd kept buried for so long? *And did any of that matter?*

As she dipped her head to taste him, one of Max's friends called out. "You two all right?"

Annabel jerked her head up to spot Goatee Man, Gabe, and Tim heading straight toward them.

Stifling a sigh, Max crawled out from under her and lifted her to her feet.

"Do you need a doctor?" Tim asked. "Wait here, Annabel. Gabe, go get—"

"No, no, I'm fine." She ducked her head and brushed herself off. "How about you, Max?"

"Never better." His smirk telegraphed a thousand possibilities.

"What were you doing back here?" Dick asked. "I thought you were going to round up the troops."

"I got distracted." Max shrugged. "So sue me."

"Aw, I'll let it pass this time. I can understand you wanting to swing with a pretty girl instead of rounding up that bunch of roughnecks. But if you're finished showing off for your new girlfriend, we need to rock 'n' roll."

Annabel stooped down to retie her boot and hide her rosy red cheeks. She hadn't been called a "pretty girl" since she was six. She sure wasn't Max's girlfriend, and she hadn't been discovered in such an awkward position since—well, since last night at Music Hall. Darn, she'd been right about Max being a bad influence.

"Do I have time to step into the ladies' room before we go?" She brushed off the knees of her jeans and tried to pull herself together. "I'm probably a mess."

Max tugged on a curl that tickled her cheek. "You look great all ruffled and touchable, but we have time if you want to freshen up."

"Don't you have the damnedest luck?" Dick asked Max as Annabel hurried ahead of them toward the Blue Moon. The men followed a few steps behind her, but their voices carried on the breeze. "Seems like every time I turn around, women are throwing themselves at you."

"Yeah," Gabe agreed, "but this is the first time you've ever bothered to catch one."

At the next stop, Max left Annabel in Dick's safekeeping and slipped away from The Dockside Tavern. He followed a path through the tangle of brush that hugged the riverbank. If he judged the location right, he'd emerge near the boat ramp where he should have met Mercer fifteen minutes ago.

Keeping a couple hundred bikers on schedule was never easy, but punctuality wasn't the snitch's strong suit either. Money was the only language Mercer spoke. He'd either be there or he wouldn't, depending on what other offers had materialized.

Quietly making his way to the meeting place, Max found Mercer waiting as promised. Slumped down in his ten-year-old Caddy, the informer smoked a stogie and listened to a Reds game on the radio. He'd grumbled about driving all the way out here, but Mercer refused to be caught anywhere near Max in Cincinnati.

"You got it?" Max asked with a rap on the roof of the car.

"Yeah, I got it," the snitch growled, squinting at Max through a haze of cigar smoke. "You got my money?"

Max pulled an envelope out of an inside jacket pocket.

"Here's half. Let's see what you got before you get the rest."

"I should get double for this." Mercer handed over a memory stick. "Gasoline don't come cheap, you know."

"I'll need to see it."

"I know, I know." The snitch tapped into a small laptop, then took back the memory stick and slid it into place. "Look at this."

With a low whistle, Max scanned documents that revealed the double-bookkeeping records on an equipment scam in city acquisitions. "Just a little more and I can shut these jerks down. If you can get to me *before* the next operation, I'll triple your fee."

Beads of sweat formed on Mercer's flat forehead. "Oh, man, you don't know what you're asking."

"Sure, I do."

"That could cost me my job."

"Nah, I'll protect you as a source. And if I can get pictures independent of this evidence, half the mooks in your department will land in jail and you'll probably get promoted." Max grabbed the memory stick and tucked it in his pocket, then extracted the other half of the payment.

Mercer ran a hand over his bristly chin while he wrestled with his decision. As Max expected, greed won out.

"I'm not promising, but I'll text you if I hear anything." He dropped the money on the seat beside him and started the land yacht.

"By the end of the week," Max prompted.

"Nah, that's too soon. Maybe next week." Mercer threw out his cigar butt with the less-than-original parting shot, "Don't call me, I'll call you."

The whole transaction took about two minutes. And not spending any more time with the slimy Mercer than that pleased Max just fine. He preferred to get back to Annabel before Tim tried to move in on her again. She was no match for the innocent-looking smile his buddy used to disguise his hit-and-run tactics.

Max turned to head back to The Dockside. His step faltered as he discovered Annabel standing at the edge of the trees watching him. She'd removed her jean jacket, showing off how well her tidy body filled out her T-shirt and jeans. With her hair scraped back in a ponytail again and her lips pursed thin like Tinker Bell in a snit, she looked anything but happy to see him.

Although now that he knew her a little better, he detected a hint of excitement behind her ocean-blue eyes.

"All right." She crossed her arms and tapped her foot. "What's really going on?"

"What do you mean?" Max closed the gap between them in six long strides. He wrapped his arms around her and pulled her against him. Partially as a distraction, but also due to inclination.

"I mean, we keep stopping at all these seedy places where members of your group come out with secret contents in little white envelopes. Guys talk openly about drug deals. You sneak away to make contact with some shady character." She pushed back and looked him square in the eye. "Do we run the risk of getting busted, should I call the police, or what?"

*Call the police? Hell, no!* Mercer would bolt like lightning if knew he'd been spotted with Max, let alone aroused enough suspicion to warrant dragging in the police. Max would have to tread carefully to determine what Annabel had seen.

"Morgan, you wound me." He clutched his hands to his heart as if to staunch the flow of blood, then flashed her his most-winning grin. "Does this mean you don't trust me? Or that you aren't having a good time?"

"No, I mean, yes. I mean, we're still shaky in the trust department, but I am having a good time." She opened her eyes wide and smiled, as if the admission surprised her. It sure as hell surprised him. "Despite my expectations, the bikers are really nice. Even though I know I'll be sore tomorrow, I love riding on the motorcycle. I'd love—" She waved a hand in the air, erasing her show of enthusiasm. "Don't try to change the subject."

"What was the subject?" He scratched his chin. "You want to know about the white envelopes, huh? If you promise not to tell anyone, I'll show you mine." He pulled one out of a back pocket and handed it over. "This information is top secret. You ready?"

She took it from him, opened the flap gingerly and peeked inside. She frowned and wrinkled her brow as she pulled out three ordinary playing cards. "What are these?"

"It's the nine-jack-queen of diamonds." He clasped her hand and steered her toward the Dockside. "And if we don't get back before Dick's ready to pull out, I won't get my card for this stop."

"But why are you getting cards? What will you do with

them?"

"It's a poker run, darlin'. I thought you knew."

"Knew what?"

"Poker runs are planned rides motorcycle clubs make to support a local charity." He took the cards from her and shoved them back in his pocket. "Didn't you see the sign at the first stop that said 'Ride a bike, feed a tyke?'"

"I guess so."

"All our rides are for charity. That's why they named this group the Good Riders. Today's ride benefits the Feed a Child Foundation, but Dick gets a kick out of making the theme rhyme whenever he can. When we register, we pony up a hundred bucks each, then we ride a designated route that no one but Dick knows in advance. We stop at seven predetermined spots to pick up a card. At the end of the day, the rider who can put together the best poker hand splits the jackpot with the charity. And right now, I'm holding the better part of a straight flush."

Annabel mulled over that information. "Is that good?"

"Yeah, it's real good."

"Oh." She looked a little deflated by the knowledge that some of their activities weren't as wicked as she'd imagined. "And you have a patch that says you're Awesome Good because..."

"I've ridden over fifty thousand miles for charity."

"And raised a lot of money, I guess. That *is* awesome." She had to give him that, but she added a little sniff. "Gambling. Is that legal?"

He laughed. "Is bingo legal? Or the lottery? It's the same kind of thing."

He kept ahead of her on the overgrown path, holding back branches and limbs. When they reached a clearing, they walked openly through the field, instead of stealthily, as Max had traveled earlier in the opposite direction. Her hand in his was small and delicate, almost getting lost inside his much larger, rougher one.

"What about the drug dealers?" The stubborn lift of her chin indicated she wasn't about to be distracted from her suspicions.

"I don't know anything about any drug dealers," Max admitted honestly. "Sometimes new guys come and try some shit, but Dick runs a pretty tight ship. He'd throw them out on their asses or call the cops himself before he'd let something like that go. Do you know who they were? What were they selling? And who were they trying to sell it to?"

"I'd recognize them if I saw them again. One of them was trying to get someone called Bruno to score some drugs for him."

"Bruno, huh?" He exaggerated a huge yawn to keep from laughing. Her eagerness to find intrigue where none existed amused the hell out of him. "I guess I'm not surprised."

"Shouldn't we tell somebody? Like Dick? Or the police?"

"Not yet."

"Well, what are we going to do?"

He hooked his arm around her neck and pulled her close enough to whisper into her ear, "I'm an investigative reporter, darlin'. We'll do a little investigatin'."

"We will? Me, too?" Her eyes got huge at the prospect. "How?"

"Keep your eyes open, and we'll nose around and see what we can find out."

"Is that what you were doing just now?"

"When?"

"When you were talking to that guy in the Cadillac."

He didn't mind pulling her leg a little about Bruno. Anything that happened in that direction would be harmless, but he didn't want her to have any hint of his deal with Mercer. That arrangement encompassed real danger, and Max would use any distraction available to steer her away from his source. "I'm not allowed to say."

"Why not? Are you working on a story? Was he an informant?" She put a finger to his lips. "And don't try to mislead me again."

"All right, I'll kiss you instead."

"Why would you do that?" She pulled her finger away from the gentle nip of his teeth. "You don't even like me very much."

"I like kissing you." Max couldn't think of a better way to distract her. Besides, having her so near reminded him of the end of their date the night before. He wanted to wipe all memory of that last sissy little peck she'd given him right out of her head.

"That's not enough." She sidestepped the arm he tried to

place around her and glanced toward the tavern.

"Not enough for what?"

"Enough to base a relationship on."

"I don't want a *relationship*, darlin'." He took an involuntary step away from her, as if just the mention of the word carried airborne germs.

"Oh, well, good. Just so we're both on the same page."

As if kissing might lead to a relationship. Nobody knew better than he did that the physical stuff was just for fun. Kissing with your clothes on was the prelude to nude foreplay. He left all that emotional hogwash to people with dependency issues. He knew who he was, and what he liked, and right now, he'd like to kiss this woman and strip her naked. He curled his fingers around her upper arms and pulled her close.

Her eyes danced with amusement, and he realized she'd been teasing *him* for a change. He caught just a glimpse of her smile before his mouth covered hers. She tasted like peppermint, of all things, and he discovered he loved peppermint.

He licked her bottom lip, and she nibbled his. Running her fingers through his hair, she massaged his scalp. His hands traveled her spine and tingled their way to the small of her back. The heat that had been building as he sat between her thighs on the bike fed his desire and encouraged him to touch all the soft and curving places that had taunted him throughout the day.

He inched up her T-shirt until he stroked the warm skin of her back. One hand moved its way up her side, stopping at the silky barrier of her bra. The damn things should be against the law.

His mouth trailed across the softness of her cheek to her delicately shaped, delicious ear, and then down her long, apparently, extremely sensitive neck. She moaned, she groaned, and she pressed against him. Oh, baby.

As he nudged her shirt away from her collarbone with his chin, he caught a glimpse of a lemon-yellow bra strap. Wondering if it had a front or back clasp, he made up his mind to find out.

"Oh, ooh," she sighed.

"Oh, yeah."

"Oh, God... Roger!"

"What?" Max continued nibbling. "The name's Max, darlin'."

"No, it *is* Roger." She straightened and pulled away as she pointed over his shoulder. "What's your shooter doing here?"

Max scowled and turned to see the cameraman strolling toward them, camera-aimed. "You mean, besides interrupting?"

"Hey, guys, don't stop on my account," Roger said. "This is a lot better than anything I got last night. Want to use it for Tess's show?"

"Don't you dare." Annabel scrambled to tug her clothes back into place.

"Sure," Max said at the same time, then amended, "If it's not going to air, I'll take a copy for my own private collection." He waggled his eyebrows and leered like a dirty old man, which earned him a punch on the arm from Annabel.

"I thought you'd be here sooner," she said to Roger.

"Who me?" The cameraman pointed a meaty finger toward his chest. "I've been around. Sometimes it's good to go unnoticed. Mostly I've been getting some long shots, candid shots. Ate at The Blue Moon. Got some good footage of the thing at the swing." He gave Max an admiring look. "Nice going."

Annabel gasped. "You shot that? Why didn't you let us know you were there?"

"Max knew."

She wheeled around to glare at Max. "Why didn't you tell me?"

Before she could really dig in her heels and refuse to move, he gathered her to his side and started forward. "I told you he'd show up sometime. I knew he was at The Blue Moon somewhere. I didn't know the pervert was watching us during the swing thing."

"It was spontaneous, not staged?" She nibbled on the bottom lip he'd been sucking just a minute before.

"If you think I've planned any of the stuff that's happened between us, then you give me credit for a greater command of the universe than I actually have. I'm totally winging it here."

A light bulb practically went off beside her head. "Roger's not here because of us! He's here to get video on the drug bust."

"Annabel," Max said firmly. "He's here because of *Let's Talk*. There is no other story. There is no drug bust. I'll prove it to you when we rejoin the group."

"Right." She didn't look or sound convinced. "He's not

here *just* because of us. Look at that long lens he's got on his camera. It's capable of shooting a lot better image from a greater distance than the smaller one he used last night."

"Maybe it's a slow news day and he came out to tape a human interest piece on the bikers for the news at six. Is that it, Rog?"

"Yeah, that's it." Good old Roger never let Max down. "Are you and these other born-to-be-wild maniacs ready to head out on the highway?"

# Chapter Six

After another two-hour race into the future, Annabel left Max waiting in line for his next card while she hobbled to the restroom. Her legs still wiggled like cooked noodles occasionally, but she didn't mind so much anymore.

Much to her surprise, she loved the exhilarating freedom of riding on the motorcycle. She loved the wind rushing past her. She loved watching the scenery fly by in a swirl of color. And to be honest, she loved clinging to Max and hugging his rock-hard thighs between hers.

She regretted not shedding her all-too-sensible tendencies long before this. The ideas and visual images for the biker documentary kicking around inside her head could wait another day. Tomorrow, her humdrum, responsibility-laden life returned. But today, she'd live it up.

She'd go to the ball like Cinderella. She'd rub elbows with a motorcycle gang, drug dealers, and—best of all—with mad, bad, and dangerous-to-know Max Williams.

She'd be fun, funny, and flirtatious.

Maybe.

She'd try her darnedest to be wild, free, and daring.

But only a little, she amended, as she washed squished bugs off her visor.

She might dabble with playing with fire, but she didn't want to get burned, and Max was a raging inferno. Just the memory of his kiss packed enough heat to set her hair aflame. Another kiss like the last one and she'd spontaneously combust.

She resolved not to miss a thing when the drug bust went down. An undercover story could vanish with the first hint of suspicion. Of course, Max had to act like there wasn't anything going on. Keeping a close eye on him for the rest of the afternoon wouldn't be a hardship.

Maybe she'd reveal a hidden flair for covering real news stories. Out of instinct, she'd copied down the license plate number of the Cadillac Max had snuck off to meet.

Yep, this could send her career in a whole new direction.

Leaving the restroom, she looked around for Bruno or Ponytail Guy. Bruno, in his blue bandana, lurked at the edge of the parking lot talking to Dick and another suspicious-looking dude with a buzz cut and steely eyes. His cold, scary eyes gave her the shivers even from five feet away. When he flipped open his leather jacket to reach for a pack of cigarettes, Annabel glimpsed a gun tucked into a shoulder holster. She stifled a gasp.

With an anxious glance, she located Max not too far away, checking over his bike and chatting with Roger.

Max smiled when he spotted her looking his way. Putting her finger to her lips, she motioned him over.

"What?" he whispered.

"Look." She jerked her chin toward Dick and the pair of suspects. "It's one of the drug dealers talking to Dick. The other one is carrying a concealed weapon. Let's get closer so we can hear what's going on."

Max crossed his arms and studied her, scowling instead of heaping praise or approval on her for her keen detecting skills. "I could let you go on like this indefinitely, you know, but I guess I won't. Come on."

"Where?"

"I'm going to introduce you to your drug ring."

"But—But—"

"Just follow my lead." He circled her wrist with his fingers and pulled her along with him to the trio of men. "How's it going, Bruno? Kirby." He nodded to both men. "I don't think either one of you have met Annabel Morgan. Annabel, this is Dan Kirby. He's a detective with the Cincinnati Police Department." Max's eyes twinkled as he headed off her next question. "Vice, not Narcotics."

"Detective Kirby." Beginning to comprehend the extent of her mistake, she considered hiding behind a tree before the conversation went any further.

"Ma'am." The detective took her measure with a flick of his eyes.

"One of my neighbors is on the Vice Squad," she said. "Jim Dennison? You know him?"

"Maybe," Kirby grudgingly allowed. Just like Jim, Kirby had mastered holding his cards close to his chest.

Max shot her another quick grin. "And this other ne'er-do-well is Dr. Bruce Townsend, He's an immunologist doing AIDS research at the University.

"It's a pleasure to meet you, Doctor." She swallowed back a big dose of embarrassment. "That's a fascinating field."

Bruno reached out to shake her hand. "Plenty of challenges."

"He's close to getting FDA approval on a faster-acting experimental drug that inhibits the condition with fewer side-effects."

"Wonderful," she managed to choke out as she looked around. There were trees aplenty, but now she wanted something bigger to hide behind—like a mountain. She two-stepped to the side, but Max clamped his hand onto her shoulder. He wasn't going to let her off that easy.

"No, it's *my* pleasure, but call me Bruno."

"Bruno, then."

"And did I mention that Dick is a judge?" Max asked so smugly she wanted to kick him in the shins. Or higher.

"No, I don't think you did." Her annoyance with him for misleading her made it difficult to squeeze out the words.

"Then, officially, I'd like you to meet Appellate Judge Richard T. Ubecki."

"Judge Ubecki, of course. I've seen your picture in the paper many times, but I didn't recognize you without your robes."

"You just keep right on calling me Dick. As you might guess, we don't stand on ceremony here. To keep everyone on the same footing, we leave our titles at home."

"You look a little shell-shocked there, Annabel." Max rubbed a hand up and down her spine, and she jerked away. "Something wrong?"

"N-no." She felt winded but determined to stand her ground and own up to her mistake—somewhat. "I guess I had the wrong impression of what kind of people ride Harleys and belong to motorcycle clubs."

"Common mistake," Bruno said.

"You should see the way people race to lock up their valuables when we pull into a small town," Detective Kirby said. "And we bring more law enforcement with us than they could muster on their best day."

"Contrary to the media stereotype," Dick added, "most of us aren't rebels or outlaws. We ride to get away from the stress of our jobs and raise money for local charities—not to loot or terrorize the locals."

"After the risks some of us take at work," Bruno put in, "this seems tame in comparison."

"Spending the day with you has sure opened my eyes." Annabel prayed they'd never know how blind she'd been.

"I hope you've enjoyed yourself," Bruno said. "A lot of outsiders—females, especially—don't like to come to these all-day events."

"Usually a two-hour ride is as long as my wife can last, bless her heart," Dick said.

"You've sure been a good sport, Annabel," the detective praised. "Come ride with us again anytime."

"First, we have to finish this one." Max glanced at his watch.

"Spread the word to mount up." Dick's voice rang with authority she now recognized sprang from the courtroom and not from the life of a drug lord or biker chieftain.

As she climbed up behind Max, Annabel left the visor of her helmet up. She needed to let the wind blow the rest of her misconceptions out her head.

"It's not a big deal," Max told her at the end of the day. The whole group had circled back to The Hoghouse for a post-ride bonfire and pig roast. "None of them knew what you were thinking."

Standing with Max in line for the delicious-smelling food being cooked in the open air, the flames from the roaring fire threw additional heat onto her cheeks. She pressed her palms over them again, knowing she deserved the laughter he tried to suppress.

"Come with me." He cupped her elbow. Guiding her away from the food, the fire, and the ready-to-party riders, he led her through the cool air and down a path to a lookout over the river.

The softness and romance of twilight crept around them, but she barreled right through it, focused on her inner turmoil. "You told me to keep an open mind, but did I? No-oo." She cringed again. "I wanted to behave less sensibly—not senselessly."

"Don't beat yourself up. Some of them dress and act the stereotype to promote the image on purpose. It gives them a chance to break loose and forget they spend their weekdays as one of the suits, kissing corporate asses and playing by the rules."

"You don't."

He studied the river undulating around the bend, then turned to lean against the rail. "Everybody does in some way or another."

"Maybe so, but I wanted to fit in with the club. I thought I was on the adventure of my life, and I wanted them to like me." She wanted *him* to like her. "But I had to start judging them, looking for a way to keep them at arm's length. What an idiot I am." Pacing back and forth, she pounded one hand with the other.

"Are you done yet?" Max hid a yawn behind his hand.

She'd expected him to react with jokes or sympathy or even logic, not boredom or impatience. Embarrassed by her outburst, she stopped pacing and studied her toes. "I guess."

He pulled her around to face him and lifted her chin on his finger. "Annabel, most people accept you at face value. If you're aloof and snooty, that's how you'll be treated. Today, you looked and acted like a normal person, not like someone above having a good time. You made mistakes, but you didn't poker up or demand to be taken home or call the police, any of the things the regular Annabel would have done."

She closed her eyes, embarrassed to admit, "I thought about doing all those things."

"But you didn't, and the people here liked your attitude. You heard them ask you to come again."

"I thought they were just being nice."

"Don't count on it. There've been lots of guests who started a ride and called for someone to come get them at the first stop. You gutted it out, and everyone respects that."

"Do they?" *Do you?*

"Sure, even me."

"Thank you." His comment raised her spirits, as if she'd earned a gold medal. Thinking back over the day, she let herself feel a little bit proud of how far she'd stepped out of her usual parameters. There was one thing she still wondered about though. "I still haven't figured out how the silver Cadillac fits into the day's events."

"Not in any way you need to know about." Max's voice hardened and cut through the space between them. "Forget you ever saw that, okay?"

*Not likely.* The license number burned a hole in her pocket. Watching him closely, she detected no humor in the grim set of his mouth. Well, okay, then. She could take a hint. Best to change the subject. "At least, I didn't suspect *everybody* I met of dealing drugs."

His eyes crinkled up at the corners again. "Who did you exclude?"

"A couple of people I talked to while you skulked off to your secret meeting. I met a nice trauma nurse named Janice Winston. And Larry Munson. His daughter goes to school with Carly."

"Like I said, Good Riders are just regular people with a hobby."

"That gorgeous fireman seemed above reproach."

Max's eyes narrowed. "Because he was gorgeous?"

"No, because he was nice. Is he single?"

"He's new to the club. I don't know much about him, but I'll find out for you, if you're interested." He spit the words out.

"No, just curious." She smiled a little, tickled by his annoyance. "I liked Dick, Tim, and Gabe, too."

Max snorted. "Just how over-protected were you growing up?"

"I didn't get out much, but they're your friends, and I thought they seemed nice."

"Dick's great. A handy guy to know, and he's been married to the same woman forever. Gabe's a champ. He works in marketing at P&G and he's a computer genius. Everybody likes him, and he just got engaged to a real looker. But watch out for Tim. He's a shark. Financial and otherwise."

With the sun dipping below the horizon, the temperature cooled noticeably. Annabel wished for the jacket she'd left on the bike. She crossed her arms and hugged them against herself to ward off the chill. "I thought he was your friend."

"He is. Pretty good one, too." He draped an arm around her and pulled her close, enveloping her in his warmth. "But that doesn't mean I'd want one of my sisters to go out with him."

Craning her neck a couple of inches back, she peered all the way up at him. "How many sisters do you have?"

"Two."

Why did that surprise her? It wasn't like she knew everything there was to know about him. Actually, she didn't know much, but he seemed so independent. She couldn't quite picture him with a regular group of relatives—parents, siblings, cousins. "Where do they live?"

"Nashville."

"Where you're from?"

"Yes, ma'am."

"Well, that explains the mysterious drawl you take on and off like a pair of sunglasses."

"All the big news markets expect their reporters to sound like everyone else." He grimaced. "When I'm not on-camera, some of the Southern-ese tends to creep back in."

"Mostly when you're being a tease."

"Do I tease you?" The finger he trailed along her cheek did just that.

"All the time." She leaned in the other direction, away from the inclination to wrap herself around him. "But I'm on to that trick."

Accepting her withdrawal, he held up his hands and shoved them into his pockets. Unfortunately, the move took all of his glorious warmth away, too. "Dang, soon you'll be on to all my little secrets."

"Do you have many?"

His shrug was all shoulders. "No more than most."

But he did and excelled at hiding them behind a mask of nonchalance and a killer smile more cleverly than she hid hers behind old-maid clothes or in the editing room. "Tell me about your family. Do you have parents?"

Bleak shadows flickered behind his eyes. "Doesn't everybody?"

"No."

He rubbed the back of his neck with his hand. "Well, yeah, okay. My mother split when I was four. Dad gave up a promising music career to sell insurance during the week and pump gas on the weekend to keep us fed."

"Where are they now?"

"I hear Ma's running a health club in Florida with her third or fourth husband. Dad's retired, still in Nashville, bouncing grandkids on his knee and picking up the occasional gig on the weekend."

"Sounds nice." Annabel's older sister hadn't been back to Cincinnati in years, and they'd never been close. If she didn't have Carly, she'd have no one but a prickly aunt from her father's side and some scattered cousins on her mother's.

He frowned. "On what planet?"

"Mine, I guess. Messy, maybe, but real. Life at my house was very serene." At least, on the surface. "Sterile. Isolated."

"What happened with your folks?"

"My parents were professors at the University of Cincinnati. Mother was philosophy. Father, literature. They spent lots of time reading and thinking deep thoughts." She mulled over how much or how little of her stifling home life to reveal. "My childhood memories include years of stiff propriety and polite indifference followed by lingering illness."

"Any sisters and brothers?"

"One sister, Elaina. Older."

"Is she as...um, conservative and responsible as you?"

"No, they were nearly forty when they adopted her, and she turned out to be a handful. A few years later, much to her surprise, Mother got pregnant with me. By then, Elaina's liveliness had exhausted their limited supply of parental energy. I countered that by being as little trouble as possible. She left to study art in Europe after high school. I stayed home to care for our ailing mother. Not long before she died, Father fell ill, too."

"Tough break." The arm he'd removed a few minutes before crept back around her, pulling her close and warming her up again. "What would you have done instead, if you'd had the choice?"

"Film school in New York." She didn't hesitate with her response, but lately she wondered if she would've had the guts to take such a big risk. Would she have braved going out on her own in the big city?

He grunted in understanding. "Is that why there weren't any boyfriends? You were too busy nursing your parents?"

"Yes, but even before that... they were very strict with me. I guess they thought they were too lenient with Elaina, so I wasn't allowed to go out much. When I did, I never fit in with the other kids. Kind of like today."

"You fit in." He grinned. "Sort of."

"You know I was out of step all day. Everybody but me knew what was going on. And I blew several unrelated, innocent incidents all out of proportion."

"Maybe I should've clued you in sooner than I did." At least he had the grace to admit that

"Yes, you should have, you rat." She gave him a half-hearted punch in a very muscular arm. "You knew what I'd assume as soon as you said we were going somewhere with a motorcycle gang."

"I said *club*, not gang."

"How was I supposed to know the difference?" She pushed against his immovable shoulder, trying to put a little space between them.

She expected him to push her back. Instead, he pulled and brought her against his broad chest with a thump.

"So." He laced his fingers together at the nape of her neck. "Did you like my idea of a good time?"

"Yes," she admitted. "I would never have picked it, but it was fun."

"You want to try it again?"

The intensity of how much she wanted to try it again frightened her. He made her want to do things, feel things, take risks she'd never attempted before. For one day, it had been fine. But did she dare continue? With a sinking heart, she didn't think so.

She opened her mouth to tell him so, but before the refusal escaped, his lips covered hers. Gentle, at first, then firmer and more demanding, the kiss managed to suck all thought from her head, all air from her lungs, all good intentions into the vapor. She leaned into him as he pulled her closer, spinning helplessly from the sexual chaos he created inside her.

His strong arms enveloped her. Hands moved everywhere. Hers along his ribs, and his under her T-shirt. Years of suppressed desire exploded within her. Textures that had never seemed so vivid before, so erotic, now provided sensations that took her to the edge. The soft denim of his shirt and the rasp of his jaw incited her with a need so great she forgot who she was, who he was, and where they were.

The heat that engulfed her didn't abate as he lifted her shirt and the evening breeze caressed her breasts. His hands skimmed the lace cups of her bra and drew a groan of pleasure from her. As his head bent forward to tease her nipple with his tongue, cheering erupted from down the hill.

"Oh my God." She tugged on the hem of her shirt. "Can they see us?"

"No." He held her against him with his hands at her waist. "They're probably announcing the winning poker hand."

A tug of war developed over the position of her shirt. For every inch he tried to raise it, she pulled it down two. "We can't do this here."

"Fine." He surrendered her shirt. The soft warmth of his breath nuzzled her neck and lulled her into momentary acquiescence. "We could go to my place."

"Why?" She sounded like the world's biggest dummy as the word emerged from her mouth and his meaning dawned on her. Full on heat washed through her as she pictured going to his apartment and opening herself up to the kind of pleasures she knew he could provide.

She wanted to, oh, how she wanted to, but she knew herself well enough to know she'd never be able to indulge in such a carnal encounter with someone as worldly as Max. Everything about the idea scared her to death. She would be overwhelmed by him, and he would find her lacking in so many ways. Setting aside her regrets, she gathered herself together and gave him the good manners her mother had taught her. "Oh, no. I couldn't, but thank you for the offer."

"Don't go all Martha Stewart on me." He looked at her with eyes that sharpened to clear focus from the blurry haze of passion. "Just tell me why not."

"I'm flattered. Maybe." Having never been propositioned by someone with his reputation, she couldn't be sure how she did feel. Flattered that he wanted her. Intimidated that his desire included so many others. Insulted that she was just one more in a long line of easy women who succumbed to his charms. "But it won't work. We're nothing alike. We're too different. We want different things."

"You wanted the same thing I did a few seconds ago." His fingertips stroked the base of her neck, urging her to reconsider.

With each passing second, she grew colder. "I changed my mind."

"All I want is for you to go home with me for the night. I'm not asking for a lifetime commitment."

"Well, that's good." She forced false cheerfulness into her tone. "Because I'm not interested in anything serious."

"You think I am?" His voice rumbled with incredulity.

"No, no, I know I'd just be another bump in the road for you." She paused for a denial, but forged on when he didn't offer one. "But you're a distraction I can't afford right now. It's time for me to concentrate on my career." It sounded lame even to Annabel, and as the warmth of his hand dropped away from her neck, she almost recanted.

"That's bull, but that's fine." He turned on his heel and started down the path toward the party. "You tell yourself whatever you want."

"It's nothing personal." She raced to catch up with him.

"Sure, it is, Morgan. It's very personal, but don't worry. I could take it as a compliment. I didn't realize you found me that fascinating. I've known women who wanted to use me as a stepping-stone in their careers, but no one's ever considered me an obstacle before. In fact, if you'd played your cards right, I might have been able to help you out." The accompanying shrug was as indifferent and as insulting as the insinuation.

As if she would ever sleep with someone to get ahead!

As if she needed to!

Other women in his life might be opportunistic and ambitious enough to climb into bed with him to advance their careers, but she had stronger principles than that. She had the talent and self-confidence to take her where she wanted to go. She didn't need Max Williams and his mind-numbing kisses.

She didn't need him at all.

She'd show him how much she didn't need him.

He'd see when she won the Community First award right in front of his nose.

Her indignation carried her down the path and all the way home. Having acquired a feel for the bike on the long day's journey, she held herself erect in a Max-free zone and slammed into him only when he braked in front of her house.

"Here you are," he said as she scrambled to put a space between them big enough to hold a truckload of differences. "Safe and sound again at home." His vanilla voiceover tones contained no sarcasm or emotion, but somehow she knew his impassivity hid a sneer. "Just the way you like it."

"Thank you." She snapped the helmet into place on the back of the seat, determined to remember her manners even though he remained planted on the Harley. "I had an interesting day."

"Good." Not very encouraging.

Honestly, she couldn't say she hoped they'd do it again sometime. But now that she looked at life from the safe vantage point of her own sidewalk, the idea of driving around tamely in her Saab for the rest of her life did seem rather—flat.

"Well, then, thanks, again." She made herself turn and head up the walk.

"Annabel," he said, as she neared the porch.

She stopped but didn't turn back. "What?"

"Do you ever do anything spontaneously? Just because you want to?"

"I went with you today, didn't I?" She continued to face her front door and wasn't sure if he heard her.

"That you did." The Harley engine roared to life on the last word, then died out again as if he'd thought better of leaving. "But you would have stayed home if Carly and I hadn't urged you on."

She ignored the truth of his statement and swung around to confront him. "What about you? Do you ever take *anything* seriously?"

"Only my work when I have to. And my family."

The bit about his family gave her pause, but only briefly. Knowing he cared about his family raised her opinion of him. Not enough to bridge the gap between them though. A close-knit family and winning personality didn't make up for pregnant ex-girlfriends, one-night stands, strippers, and the downfall of innocent interns. "That's why this is goodbye."

He shook his head. "That's not why. You're saying goodbye because you're tempted by everything about me and that terrifies you."

"Hah! You're as afraid of me as I am of you!"

"I'm not afraid." He flung himself off the bike and strode forward, sweeping her into his arms. His kiss consumed her in a firestorm of challenge and passion.

Annabel struggled to keep up with it. Hot and hungry. Frustrated and angry. Eager and wary. All the confusing emotions of the day poured into one heart-stopping embrace. If they continued, she might invite him inside or pull him down on the ground. But he withdrew abruptly. He cradled her face in his hands and stared at her so hard, for so long, she wished she could read his mind.

"Think about how happy you are with your life the way it is," he said at last, "and you give me a call when you're brave enough to face the truth. If I'm still around, I'll show you what you've been missing."

# Chapter Seven

Tuesday afternoon, Annabel paced outside the closed doors of the Arts Commission meeting room. Her boss, Howard Lasting, sat on a wooden bench. He crossed and uncrossed his lanky legs while he stared out the window and contemplated the flow of the Ohio River.

"Annabel, have a seat." Even while bored to tears, his command assumed obedience. "You're making *me* nervous, and I have nerves of steel." He yawned and closed his eyes.

Probably not a good time to broach her biker brainstorm. But she so rarely had him as a captive audience, it seemed a shame not to make the most of the opportunity. She perched on a seat across from him.

"I have an idea about a documentary on motorcycle clubs." The statement contained none of the polish she'd practiced on the way to work that morning.

"A motorcycle club?" Howard opened his eyes and looked at her with disdain. One of his bristly, caterpillar eyebrows arched upward. "Like the Hells Angels? *Easy Rider? The Wild Bunch?* Black leather jackets aside, all of that sounds so sixties."

"That's what I thought at first, too," she said. "But respectable motorcycle clubs consist of weekend warriors who ride for fun, not to rebel or make some anti-establishment social statement. You should see a pack of them roaring along the highway with gleaming helmets and chrome."

"Unh," he groaned. "I have seen one. A couple of weeks ago, a whole parade of those bozos moved through an intersection like a psychotic funeral procession, trapping me in place for ten minutes. Damned aging hippies."

"It's not like that." Not entirely. "People from all walks of life belong to them, from judges to mechanics. They get together for rallies, rides, fundraisers, and meetings. They have their own newsletters and Facebook pages, like the 4-H or the Shriners."

He rubbed a finger up and down his prominent nose, indicative of his thinking mode. "Who could we sell it to?"

Getting a paying sponsor was always the second step toward approval—right after the initial idea. When Howard turned to the bottom line, she knew she'd caught his interest. "The Motorcycle Organization of America." She jumped up to pace again as she bounced the idea toward him. "They might want to use it to spruce up their image."

"Maybe."

"Or motorcycle safety awareness to promote wearing helmets." She made a viewfinder with her hands and framed the mental image. "Sunlight gleaming off all those shiny acrylic heads would make a stunning visual."

Howard chuckled. She might have hooked him. "Hmmm." He rubbed his nose again.

"Or shoot it with a philanthropic angle." She continued to pace. "Did you know that some bike clubs use their rides to raise money for charity?"

"I did not know that," he said then nodded.

*Thank God.* She let out the breath she'd been holding. A nod usually meant he deemed the project worthy of consideration.

"I see the possibilities," he admitted. "Maybe Terry can do something with it."

"Terry? No way!" Annabel objected, loudly, to the possibility of handing off her project to another producer. Howard snapped a glare her way, and she modified her tone. "I mean, it was my idea. I want to do it."

"Let's see how this goes." He jerked his head toward the meeting room. "Winning on Saturday would improve your chances of overseeing future projects." Bored again, he resumed his study of the river. "Sit down. Try to contain yourself."

"Sorry." Deflated by his lack of confidence in her, she dropped onto the bench next to him. "I guess I'm on edge. This is all new to me."

"You'll do fine." His off-hand words and disinterest eroded her small store of self-esteem.

"I'm just worried about the kids." She glanced at the clock on the wall. "They were supposed to be here ten minutes ago."

A spasm of distaste crossed his face. "How many of them are coming?"

"Three. Or four." Seven, she silently amended. Or eight.

As a nominee, she'd been invited to present witnesses to testify about the impact of her project. She intended to include as many of the students who had appeared in the film as possible, both the successes and the failures. One side balanced the other and confirmed the story she'd wanted to convey.

During the four years of production for *Challenging Destiny*, Annabel found it impossible to remain aloof from the students. In real life, she couldn't help comparing the difficulties they faced in their lives to the relative ease of those lead by Carly and her friends just a few miles away. With a slight shift in birth and geography, economics and opportunity, their lives would have been switched.

After Annabel had earned their trust, the teens often turned to her for help and advice. Sometimes she'd filled the role of social worker, mentor, or confidante, and she had grown to know and care for them all. They meant much more to her now than the subjects of a film. They were friends. With the project over, many still kept in touch.

"They'll either get here or they won't." Howard's lack of concern came as no surprise. His opposition to their presence had been a sore spot between them for days.

The elevator door opened, and two of the students stepped out. Keisha, currently a college student, and Sukari, an unwed mother who hadn't managed to graduate, but planned to get her GED soon.

Sukari had her little one with her, leading the toddler by the hand. "Come on, now, Kenyon, don't make mama any later." She picked the boy up and carried him. "Sorry, Ms. Morgan. My sister didn't tell me 'til the last minute that she couldn't babysit. But my Kenyon, he's a good boy and he won't cause trouble. Will you, fella?"

Annabel welcomed both girls. "I'm glad you brought Kenyon with you, Sukari. Look how big he's gotten." Annabel tickled the baby's tummy and gave the young women hugs. "It's great to see all three of you! Come tell me how things are going."

A few minutes later, two of her young male subjects showed up. DeSean, an aspiring sound technician/record producer, smiled and hugged Annabel, always eager to please. Warren, recently released from jail on a drug charge, scowled, like a stray dog waiting for the next kick or curse. Soon Jonah, Viper, and Selena—two former gang members and a cheerleader—joined the growing group.

"I'm so pleased you're all here with me today." Annabel

picked up baby Kenyon from the floor. He pulled her hair, tugged on an earring, and stuck his fingers in her mouth before giving her a smacking kiss on the check and wiggling to get down.

Everyone else laughed at his curiosity and energy, but Howard frowned over the growing crowd. Dismissing them as beneath his attention, he pulled out his phone and began scrolling.

The volatile combination of Warren and Viper worried Annabel a bit, but she smiled and chatted, doing her best to keep the former rivals apart. The eight teens sprawled across the chairs, benches, and tables, ignoring her boss and his disdain.

The elevator doors slid open again. With her group complete, she looked up to see who else had shown up. Her pulse registered off the Richter scale at the sight of Max.

She'd spent most of the past two sleepless nights reviewing their stupid argument. Despite feeling that it was best to leave things alone between them, a happy-to-see-him smile bloomed on her face. Remembering his last words to her, she wiped it from her mouth faster than smeared lipstick.

She doubted she ranked high on his list of favorite people these days either. But of course, when had she? Saturday, maybe. Briefly. Now, she noticed the lack of his attention the way she'd miss warm gloves on a cold winter's day.

Wearing dark pants, a charcoal sport coat, and a shirt the color of coconut cream, he looked good enough to eat. With his strong shoulders, flat stomach, muscular arms, and narrow hips, it was impossible to forget she'd spent hours snuggled up against that gorgeous display of masculinity.

But today, Annabel could only watch as a Double D bimbo with big hair and spray-on clothes clung to him like an inflatable life vest. Well, if that was the kind of woman he was attracted to... *Fine.*

"Hello, there, Morgan, Howard." He shook hands with her boss, shifted his gaze over her and ran a glance over the rest of her companions. "You've got quite a crowd here."

Her defenses rose in reaction to the quick, dismissive perusal. "Couldn't you find anyone to speak up for your project?"

"Shawntel is all I need." He patted the woman's hand and began making introductions.

Annabel's boys drooled over the bimbo's buxom display.

Even Howard seemed fascinated by the overflowing bounty. "Take my seat, Shawntel." He jumped up to make room for her.

"I guess we're early," Shawntel said in a whispery little voice. Sinking into the vacated spot, she finally released her grip on Max.

"No, the committee's running behind." Howard peeled back his cuff to check the time. "We should have been in and out of there by now."

Max practically smothered the bimbo with attention for a few moments. "Do you need a sweater? Some water? Anything?"

"I'm fine, Max." She shooed him away with a sweet smile. "Don't hover."

Satisfied she was settled comfortably, he turned to Annabel's friends. "Are all y'all here for Annabel? Nice show of support."

"Hey," Malcolm said. "You're the dude on the news."

"That's right," Keisha agreed. "I've seen you on TV. Are you here to witness for *Challenging Destiny*, too?"

"Not today." He flashed his television smile. "Although I've heard it's very good."

"Damn straight. It's got me in it, don't it?" Keisha planted an adamant fist on her hip and drew hoots of laughter from her friends.

"Then maybe I'll put in a good word for it," Max said, finally turning to Annabel. "You're looking less buttoned-down than usual, Morgan." He flicked a finger at the collar she'd left undone that morning. He seemed careful not to graze her skin, but his natural magnetism almost sucked her into his force field anyway. "Any reason?"

She clutched the top two buttons of her blouse. Years of personal self-analysis made it clear to her why she'd hidden behind her straightjacket clothes all these years. But this morning, she knew she didn't want to continue camouflaging herself that way. Max's preferences weighed not at all on the decision. *Right?*

"It's hot in here." She fanned her face with her hand.

"Like it was hot in the restaurant on Saturday?" he asked as Kenyon toddled over and tugged on his pant leg. Without hesitation, he picked the child up and tucked him into the crook of his elbow. "Hey, there, little fella."

"Ms. Morgan, Mr. Lasting," said a woman from the door. "Thank you for your patience. Please follow me."

Lynn Dorey, one of the other nominees, swept haughtily through the lobby and left with her entourage.

"Us, too?" Keisha asked.

"Not just yet." The woman took a tentative step back as she surveyed the boisterous group. "We'll call the rest of you in a little later."

Annabel stood up, indicating the place on the bench she'd just vacated. "Looks like there'll be a crowd out here for a while longer. Would you like to slip into my seat?" she asked Max.

"I'd love to slip into your seat, Annabel."

He answered her so smoothly that the innuendo didn't register until DeSean, Warren and the others laughed and elbowed one another. Even Shawntel choked back a giggle. Howard looked rather pained.

If it had been Max's intention to fluster her before her interview, she refused to let on that he accomplished it. "Come on, Howard." Annabel pulled him away from the charming Shawntel. "We're up."

🏍

Annabel's presentation went well, all things considered. At first, her nerves got the best of her, and she read from her prepared comments. But by the time the panel began questioning her, she spoke coherently and authoritatively. For his part, Howard bragged about Lasting Productions, but gave her most of the credit for the documentary.

After the students came in, the tone of the interview shifted again. They were wonderfully candid about the impact the film had on their lives. Their mature behavior and comments filled her with pride.

At the conclusion of the interview, the kids huddled around her in the waiting area, exchanging hugs and high fives. She thanked them for their participation and urged them to keep in touch even as her gaze strayed to Max.

He and Shawntel sat cozied up to one another. *Thank heavens I made the right decision and didn't sleep with him.* He had the attention span of a gnat. How mortifying it must be to occupy just another space in his long line of women.

"Let us know how the award thing turns out," DeSean said as they headed toward the elevator and stairs.

"I'll text you after the ceremony," she promised. "And good luck with your interview on Friday, DeSean."

"Thanks, Ms. Morgan, but I won't need luck." He grinned. "I'm good enough without it."

"Absolutely, but be sure to use me as a reference if you want to."

"I won't need that either." DeSean threw a salute to someone behind her. "Max knows the owner of the record company. He said he'd call and put in a good word for me."

"He did, huh?" She shouldn't resent his offer to help. Very generous, but for some reason, she felt like he'd purposely upstaged her. "Well, then, you're a shoe-in."

When Howard stopped to talk to Shawntel, Annabel decided to confront Max about making promises he didn't intend to keep. Just as she reached his side, he cursed.

"Sorry," she said, stung by the show of displeasure. "I guess this isn't the best time to talk."

He checked the screen on his phone. "I need to take this call. I'll be right back." He touched her elbow, squeezed the bimbo's knee, and strode to the other end of the hall with his cell phone in hand.

Annabel sighed and turned to Howard, ready to herd him back to work and leave all thoughts of Max Williams behind. Charley Asherton, the manager at Max's television station, had arrived at some point and now sat beside Shawntel, vying with Howard for her attention.

"Good of you to be here," Charley said to the bimbo. "Not every woman would want to be publicly identified as one of the patients in Max's series."

Annabel gave herself a mental ka-thunk to the forehead. Of course, the D-cups on display had been surgically enhanced.

"That was you?" A mix of curiosity and sympathy softened Howard's voice.

"I didn't want everyone to know my identity, but I'd do anything to help Max," Shawntel explained to the two men. "If it hadn't been for him, that butcher would still be running loose, pretending to be a competent surgeon, disfiguring other women."

"Just the botched surgeries should have been enough to have his license revoked," Charley said. "But the shoddy implants he performed on you and other women after living through the horror of mastectomies... Well, that was more than incompetence. It was criminal negligence."

"I wasn't getting anywhere with the proper legal channels," she explained. "If Max hadn't done his series, it might have been years before my case got in front of the medical review board and the courts." Shawntel looked at Annabel, who cringed inwardly. She felt like a prize idiot. Again.

She had dismissed Max's series as a forum for strippers and showgirls who wanted to increase their chest size. Why hadn't she realized the piece was about breast cancer patients? How Max must have laughed at her narrow-minded, ill-informed attitude.

"At first," Shawntel continued, "he didn't want to use my specific case in the series, but I kept after him. You know how he is about family. He can never refuse any of us anything."

"You're family?" A sharp sense of relief pricked the back of Annabel's brain, mixing with even greater humiliation.

Shawntel nodded. "We're cousins. Didn't you know? Everyone used to say we looked alike. I guess that was before I became a blonde."

"Yes, of course." Waves of shame from her unkind and suspicious thoughts swamped Annabel. "There's a definite resemblance."

"How's your health now?" Charley asked Shawntel. "Max said you're still in remission, and your last reconstruction surgery was more successful."

"Ye-es." She bit her cotton candy pink lip. "But I'd rather not talk about it."

"Of course, just being here is bound to wear you out." Charley patted her hand. "Have you gone back to work yet?"

"Part-time." Shawntel smiled brightly. "The sick leave policy at the library is excellent. The library administrator has been very understanding about letting me work shorter hours until I get back to full strength."

"You work at the library?" Oh, dear God, just kill me now.

Shawntel nodded. "I'm a reference librarian at the Oakley branch. Be sure and call me if you ever need something researched. I'm always happy to help a friend of Max's."

Annabel was spared the task of finding her voice as the door opened again and one of the committee members peered out.

"I thought Mr. Williams was here," the woman said. "We're ready for his presentation."

"I'm here, Dottie." Max strolled up as if on cue. "Everybody ready?" As he went to Shawntel's side, his solicitous attitude toward his cousin took on a whole new meaning.

Just when Annabel thought he'd ignore her completely, he stopped in front of her. "Too bad we didn't get a chance to have that talk you wanted. See you around, I guess."

"Max..." Annabel began as he turned away. "Will you call me later? There's something I want to discuss with you."

His smile turned up the heat. "Did you rethink your position about what's missing in your life?"

She should have known he'd think that. "No, it's not about that. I'd like to talk to you about something else."

"Sure, Morgan, I'll call you." Not much warmth in his gaze. She could hardly blame him.

"You just sit by the phone and wait, all right?"

*Right.* Her heart sank as she watched him walk away.

That night at the gym, Max moved through a set of crunches, trying to remember the last time a woman had turned him down flat. Just because none leaped to mind before Annabel didn't mean it hadn't happened. And he normally made a point of not hitting on women who found him repulsive.

He moved through each stage of his workout trying to remember he had bigger things to worry about than the fact Annabel Morgan refused to sleep with him. But thoughts of her kept intruding.

He'd known for years she found him about as appealing as a slug, and he'd never bothered to improve her impression of him.

When they'd first met, her intelligence, her focus, and her single-minded attention to detail had intrigued him. But when she'd turned her attention his way, she'd shown him nothing but disapproval.

True, there'd been that unfortunate incident with the intern and the rumors about him and DeeDee, but Annabel had assumed the worst from the start. She'd treated him with a prison warden's lack of humor. All business, all the time. Which tended to bring out the worst in him. Like an ass, he'd encouraged her poor opinion.

But now, her contempt tended to rankle more than when the feeling went both ways. Now he knew she was more than the frosty, unimaginative fishwife she presented to the world. When had he first noticed that natural sexiness she guarded so carefully?

Saturday, maybe, at the concert. Or Sunday, when she flew out of that swing and into his arms.

With his teeth clenched through his second set of curls, he decided to ignore all of their dissimilarities and just accept the attraction that rammed him in the gut like a sledgehammer. Hell, life was a series of risks. What was one more?

But Annabel disliked risks.

She detested them.

Her life had been one big restrictive cocoon. She'd done nothing but play it safe from the day she was born.

And if she smiled and laughed more with him than she'd smiled and laughed in the past twenty years, apparently that didn't impress her enough to tempt her away from her boring, safe, confining existence. Somewhere in her personal code of conduct, Thou Shalt Not Enjoy Life must be written in big bold letters. A needlepoint throw pillow with that motto probably held the place of honor on her bed.

*Well, so what?* He drilled the punching bag with a punishing flurry of jabs. She wasn't his problem.

Damn her. There were plenty of women around who enjoyed getting naked and having fun. He should find one of them, hit the town and party all night. He needed to get stinking drunk, make a fool of himself on the dance floor, and fall into bed with a partner willing to get hotter and sweatier than he was now. He'd done it all a hundred times before. A thousand times.

And somewhere along the line, in one of the many smoky bars, dark corners, or unfamiliar bedrooms, the frantic activity had turned into a meaningless farce.

Maybe that's why he was still working out his frustration instead of responding to the admiring glances a Spandex-clad cutie on the Stairmaster kept throwing his way.

In the locker room, as he stripped down to bare skin before

stepping into the shower, he decided to call Annabel. She'd asked him to, after all. And he had a crazy idea he wanted to run by her.

But right after that, he'd head out and find some action. He knew all the right or wrong places to look.

When clean and dressed, he pulled his cell phone out of his gym bag as he made his way across the parking lot. She answered on the first ring. For a moment, he flattered himself that she'd been waiting for his call, just as he'd sarcastically suggested.

"Just a second," she said, "I'm talking to Carly."

He dropped into the driver's seat of the newly repaired Porsche and floated in the limbo inhabited by people placed on hold. Fiddling with the radio until he found the Reds game, he shoved his seat back and reclined it as far as it would go. He considered hanging up before her voice brought him back to earth.

"I'm back." She sounded a little breathless. "Sorry, but we needed to synchronize schedules."

"No problem." He'd called her, so he supposed the ball was in his court. But she'd asked him to call, so she must have something she wanted to say. "What can I do for you?"

"I like your cousin."

Surprise, surprise. She'd realized the truth about Shawntel. "Me, too."

She cleared her throat. "I want to apologize for the things I said and thought about your news series. I didn't realize—"

"Let me guess, you hadn't seen it and you figured I used the topic as a good excuse to show boobs on TV." He heard her sputter, but she didn't deny it. "And now you feel bad since you've discovered it does have some intellectual, social, and medical relevance after all."

"Well, yes."

"Admit it. You jumped to the wrong conclusion." He waited a second to add, "Again."

"You're right. I'm sorry." No excuses, no evasion.

Well, hell. He'd never been one to carry a grudge, but he hated to let her off so easy. "Just like that? You think you can judge me, my work, and everything about me, and all it takes is a few words to make it right?"

"I hope so." She hesitated. "Is there anything else I can do?"

"Probably." Now this was interesting. He could think of a number of things she *could* do. But *would* she? "I'll accept an IOU for a future favor."

"You want an open-ended, blanket IOU for a favor to be named later?"

"Yep."

"Hmmm." She took time to consider. "We have to agree the favor won't be for anything illegal, immoral, or sexual in nature."

"Now you're takin' all of the fun out of it, darlin'." He should have known she'd negotiate to keep all her familiar parameters in place. Exhaling loudly, he released the last of his anger. "And you're insulting my character again. If you don't stop, you'll owe me another apology."

"You're right. I'm sorry. Again."

"Apology accepted." He liked having the air cleared up between them. "And not all your fault. The sexploitation promos the station ran intentionally gave viewers the wrong impression."

"They were pretty sensational."

"Tell me about it. Anytime they can link sex to a story, especially during a ratings period, they do. Eating Hot Dogs Leads to Impotence. I hate those salacious leads." He'd been fighting them for years with little success.

"I know what you mean," she said. "And I've learned my lesson. You can't tell a news story by its lead-in. I'll watch and judge for myself from now on. What have you got coming up next?"

Hopefully the equipment scam, but he couldn't tell her about that one. "A human interest story about a teacher who's trying to raise funds for a school her twin sister teaches at in Mexico."

"What will they say about that?" She deepened her voice, imitating a newscaster's dramatic intonations. "Twins Caught Soliciting."

"South of the border, at that. Details at eleven." He chuckled. "Or something worse. I'll feel really bad about it, too. She's a nice lady."

"And I'll bet you donated money to support her cause."

Surprised by her perception, he held the phone away from his ear and looked at it as if he could see her that way. "Why do you say that?"

"You don't ever just report the stories. I've noticed you get personally involved and go the extra mile."

"Yeah, well, don't tell anyone."

"They don't call you The People's Reporter for nothing."

"That's just my public relations team at work." He brushed the embarrassing nickname aside.

"And in this case," she continued, "it hits the nail on the head. I've seen how people relate to you, from the wine steward at Ernesto's to Shawntel to the kids from my documentary today. For a minute there, I was afraid they'd change their mind and go in with you."

"Are you kidding? They worship you. They wouldn't have abandoned you if I'd been handing out free Beyoncé tickets."

"I'm glad we didn't put it to the test."

"Speaking of tests, how did your presentation go?"

"Pretty well." Caution laced her voice. "How about yours?"

"The same." Shawntel had knocked the judges' socks off, but no point in bragging. "Still feel like a winner?"

"Yep." Her voice sounded more desperate than confident.

"I'll regret seeing you disappointed when I win."

"Hah. I'll let you carry the trophy out to the car for me."

"Big of you. But if you should happen to be so lucky as to win, won't you have a big, strong somebody with you to do the heavy lifting?"

After a long pause she asked, "You mean like a guest? Or Carly?"

"No, not like a guest. More like an escort. Or a date."

"Ah, well, no. I had lined up someone to go with me, but they—*he* had to cancel, and then I couldn't decide whom to favor out of my stable of admirers, and now it seems like too short notice to have someone get their tux cleaned before Friday. Carly will probably go with me. She'll be happy to carry the hardware."

He needed to proceed cautiously. "I've been making the same excuses. I mean, if I ask someone to something this special, they'll read too much into it."

"You don't have a date either? What about Shawntel?" He heard the surprise in her voice.

"Charley asked her to go with him."

"At least *somebody* has a date."

"You know," he said, oh, so casually, "I've got a tuxedo all pressed and ready to go... and we're going the same place, at the same time. Think maybe we should go together?"

"On a date?" Her voice rose several octaves.

"Of course not. You made it pretty clear the other night there wasn't any point in us going out with one another again."

"We're too different." She reminded him of one of her primary excuses for not getting involved with him.

"Neither one of us want to be serious about anyone." He reminded her of another.

"We have our careers to think about."

He needed to get her back on track. "It won't be hard to think about them at the award ceremony."

"God, no. Howard keeps implying my professional future hinges on winning it." The note of tension hummed through the connection.

He'd never admit his hopes to just anyone, but he didn't mind revealing his career plans to Annabel. "Winning's kind of important to me, too."

"How so? You're already the best reporter in Cincinnati."

"There are other places besides Cincinnati."

"You said that the other night. Would you really leave?"

"For a network job?" *How could she doubt it?* "In a heartbeat. My agent thinks things are looking good, but a win at the Community First could seal the deal."

"So we both have a lot at stake."

"But in the spirit of good sportsmanship, the loser will swallow their disappointment and congratulate the winner with a smile," he suggested and upped the ante. "And a kiss."

"And the winner will commiserate with the loser," she added.

"With a kiss. And no hard feelings either way."

"So we may as well do it."

"Go together?"

"Sure. As friends?"

"As friends." He agreed to the word in principle, but in practice, he hated it.

# Chapter Eight

"Anna!" Carly hollered with her usual gusto from the foyer. "Come quick. He's here."

Annabel stepped into her shoes, smoothed her dress, fluffed her hair, located her purse, and looked around for something—anything—else to do. With nothing left undone, she ordered herself to quit stalling and get her over-dressed fanny downstairs. She was going to the award ceremony with Max. As a friend. They'd agreed on the terms.

He stood with his back to her, looking out the front door, but she could see his reflection in the glass as she descended the stairs. Was it fair for any kind of friend to look that good? What had she been thinking, agreeing to go anywhere with a tuxedo-clad Max? There should be a law against letting him loose in mixed company wearing one.

Every woman present—herself included—would want to untie that tie and remove that vest. Slowly peel that jacket off his hard body... Unfasten those studs... Slip the shirt off those broad shoulders. *Yum!*

She floated to the bottom of the stairs before he noticed. He turned toward her when the rustling of her skirt gave her away.

Or she assumed that's what did it. She'd never worn a Cinderella dress before and couldn't believe she had one on now. Originally, she'd bought a sensible black sheath to wear to the ceremony. But once she'd agreed to go with Max, she returned it for this frivolous confection she'd been secretly eyeing for weeks.

Layers and layers of diaphanous, glittery gold billowed out around her, gathered together by a wide band that suggested a deceptively tiny waist. The skimpy two strips of fabric that comprised the halter top displayed her average-sized breasts to voluptuous advantage. Carly had said Annabel looked amazing. Judging from Max's heated stare, he thought so, too, if the word "amazing" could be interpreted as "slutty princess."

"Wow, look at you." He spun his finger in a motion that directed her to turn around. "Let's see the rest of it."

She twirled for him. She actually twirled. She'd never twirled on command in her life, but Max had her wanting to do all kinds of things she'd never done before.

He made a low wolf whistle when she pirouetted to a stop in front of him. "Backless. Fantastic. You're not all buttoned up" He reached out and stroked the deceptively casual riot of curls that grazed her shoulders. The gentle caress resonated all the way down to her painted toenails. "I'm glad you left your hair down."

"Thanks. And I'm glad we decided to go to this together." She pressed a hand against the drunken butterflies stumbling around in her stomach. "I'm much more nervous than I anticipated."

"Don't be. You'll be the hottest woman there—even after I win the award."

Her laugh came out much too loud and high pitched. "Just imagine, the hottest woman there with the best-looking guy and the winner of the award. It'll be the most outstanding night of my life."

He tipped back his head, flashed his perfect white teeth, and laughed out loud, something she hadn't seen him do before. It marked a refreshing change from his on-camera smile, the charming one he used to get his way, and the mocking one that appeared when he wanted to put her in her place. Laughter made him look younger and boyishly handsome instead of worldly and smugly sexy. She relaxed a little. Maybe young and boyish she could handle. Worldly and smugly sexy scared the wits out of her.

"Well, just in case you need it, I brought you something for luck." He handed her a white florist's box he'd obviously placed on the side table earlier.

Flowers. Another first. Tears welled up in her eyes. She gulped and gave him a wobbly smile.

Carly burst through the door. "Wait 'til you see." She pointed outside. "It's the coolest thing ever."

Relieved by the interruption, Annabel yanked her emotions back in line. "Cooler than the Harley?" She pictured the repaired Porsche as tonight's mode of transportation. She hoped her dress didn't get too squished riding in it.

"Totally different, but just as cool. Ooh, and look, he brought you flowers. What kind?"

"As if you didn't know," Max said to Carly.

"He called me to see what color your dress was," Carly confided, then grinned cheekily at Max. "I just wanted to make sure you got it right."

"There was no need for a conspiracy," Annabel said to him. "You could have asked me."

"That would have ruined the surprise." The satisfaction of his smile oozed masculinity.

Her heart took another leap. "Everything you do surprises me." She reminded herself of his reputation. She shouldn't take any of this personally. Or seriously. Even so, her hands shook as she opened the box. "How beautiful. Thank you."

She lifted the corsage of ivory roses surrounded by lily of the valley out of the green paper and sniffed. The flowers smelled almost as good as her date... er, escort... er, friend for the evening.

"Yeah, they're beautiful." Her stepdaughter dismissed them after a cursory glance. "Good job, Max. Come on, Anna, I can't wait for you to see this." Carly dropped Annabel's glittery shawl around her shoulders, then led her to the door. As Annabel stepped outside, Carly spread her arms wide. "Ta dah!"

Annabel gasped at the sight of a sleek black limo parked in her driveway.

"The driver's name is Eduardo. Isn't that just scrumptious?"

The uniformed man in the traditional driver's cap stepped up and opened the rear door.

Carly ran to the car and hopped into the back seat first. "Look, there's champagne, TV, a DVD player, sound system, and everything."

Annabel lifted her brows at Max. "Champagne?"

Mischief twinkled in his eyes as he guided her to the limo. "We'll have something to celebrate afterward."

"My victory or yours?"

"Somebody's," he said. "Maybe it'll be a tie."

The scrumptious Eduardo moved to help her in, but Max wouldn't have it. His hand held her elbow and set her skin to tingling as she slid into the backseat.

"Why did you do this?" All the effort he'd made touched her so deeply she could barely speak.

Carly bounced on the seat across from Annabel. Max slid as close to Annabel as the full skirts allowed and took her hand in his. "Carly scolded me for not using the car and driver the station offered for our *Let's Talk* date."

"So you did this for her?"

"She thought you'd enjoy it." His shrug made light of the gesture, as if it was nothing. Suddenly the gesture seemed very much like something. Something important. But no, that couldn't be.

Just one more thing to check off the list of things she'd never done before. Going on a fancy date in a limo with a blistering hot guy. Check. And somehow, without mentioning any of them to him, Max was working his way down the list.

"Are you ready to go, sir?" Eduardo asked.

"As tempting as it is to be the escort of *two* beautiful women instead of one," Max said, pointing a finger at Carly, "this one has to get out."

"Already? " The winsome teen gave him her version of puppy-dog eyes. "Maybe you can drop me off at the library. We can watch TV on the way. It's almost time for *Jeopardy*."

"Nice try." Annabel smiled at her enthusiasm. "But if you're such a big fan, go watch it inside. You don't want us to be late."

"Oh, snap. I can tell when I'm not wanted." She hugged Annabel and seemed to surprise Max by hugging him, too. "Don't forget, Anna, I'm spending the night at Logan's. Call or text to let me know what happens with the award." She ducked her head back inside the door the second before the driver closed it behind her. "I hope at least one of you gets lucky tonight."

"I hope we both do." Max squeezed Annabel's hand as the limo pulled away from the curb.

And once more, she wondered just how serious he was about maintaining this friendship thing. And how serious she wanted him to be.

Max's distaste for monkey suits and the type of events that required them faded as he watched Annabel's fascination with the glitz and glamour around her. Her wide-eyed wonder provided him with the most fun he'd had with his clothes on in a long time.

Everyone who was anyone in Cincinnati rubbed elbows in the star-studded River Room at the top of the city's fanciest hotel. Politicians and philanthropists, media personalities and sports figures abounded. Half the individuals present lived in or for the spotlight. Inflated egos in the room outran the humility quotient ten-to-one.

Max tried to steer Annabel to their assigned table without fanfare, but Roger and too many other colleagues from the station were covering the event to let him go unnoticed.

Tess, the award-ceremony emcee, looked very smug at seeing Max and Annabel together. She waited until Annabel had excused herself for a moment before heading his way. The talk show hostess kept her gaze moving to make sure she gained maximum exposure from the other luminaries in the vicinity as she questioned Max about his television date with Annabel.

"Haven't you got the footage from Roger yet?" Even though his appearance on her show had started out as a promotional stunt, he felt a flash of resentment about sharing the details of what had now become a private matter.

She looked past Max to Annabel's return trek with an appraising glance. "Yes, and I saw the sparks flying, but I didn't think things would develop this quickly. Come on." She leaned over and whispered her signature line in his ear. "Tell Tess all about it."

He took a step back from the overly ripe breasts that brushed his arm and the heavy perfume that gagged him. "There's nothing to tell, Tess."

"Hmmm." She tapped a brilliant red fingernail against lips painted the same color. "I thought you said she didn't like you. The Ice Queen sure melted under the heat of your, uhm, personality, didn't she? Does she know how indiscriminately you spread your heat around?"

He groaned over the description. "She knows all about it, and I told you, it's nothing like that." He turned to follow Annabel's progress with his gaze. That gauzy dress clung to her body like sugar crystals in some places and floated around her like a cloud in others. Her charms weren't as obvious as Shawntel's or Tess's, yet Annabel drew her own share of appreciative glances. Including his old buddy Tim's.

What the hell was that snake doing here besides slithering up to flirt with Annabel? An unfamiliar and annoying prickle of disapproval stabbed him right between the eyes.

"You should call me tomorrow and—"

"Excuse me, Tess." He ignored her frown of displeasure as he hurried to rescue Annabel.

While Max picked up his pace, she sidestepped Tim's hand on her elbow, avoided the palm he tried to plant on her bare back, and withdrew from the overly gallant, slobbering wrist-kiss Tim tried to administer. Max closed in as the bastard dropped his hand to her bottom.

"Sorry, I got delayed." Max raised his voice from a few feet away.

"No problem." Annabel turned toward him gratefully, evading Tim's attempt at draping his arm around her shoulders.

"When I saw Annabel alone, I just couldn't resist—" Tim pulled back after Max turned the full force of glare on him "—the opportunity to wish her good luck tonight." He socked Max on the arm. "You, too, buddy."

"Your support means the world to me." Max socked him back, harder than necessary. "Come on, Annabel, we should take our seats."

"Great to see you again, Annabel." Tim, the rat bastard, leaned over to kiss her cheek, but met only air. She shifted away before he could make actual contact. "Maybe we can dance later."

"Maybe," Annabel allowed.

"Don't hold your breath," Max advised his buddy over his shoulder. Was it just his imagination or did she inch closer to him for protection? Max should have punched the lowlife harder. And lower. Next time he saw Tim, he'd warn the jerk to keep his paws to himself around a nice woman like Annabel.

When they arrived at their assigned table, her slimy boss, Howard Lasting, had arrived with his brittle wife. Max genuinely enjoyed every facet of the female gender, but Sylvia Lasting didn't offer much to admire. She was one of those whipcord-thin women whose sense of humor matched her appetite—non-existent. Charley Asherton and Shawntel were present, too, but they were too wrapped up in one another to be much company for anyone else.

Max couldn't see that match-up going anywhere, but Charley, a two-time loser in the marriage game, seemed awe-struck with Shawntel. Such a sweetheart, she deserved some happiness with someone who wouldn't use her and drop her. Max would make sure Charley understood the rules.

Seated next to him in her erotic princess get-up, Annabel grew quieter with each course, although she tried to hide her jitters behind a smile.

"Are you done with that?" a harried waiter asked, preparing to remove the plate of Parmesan chicken she'd mostly rearranged on her plate.

"Yes, thank you." Water sloshed over the rim of her glass as she carried it to her lips with a shaky hand.

After the untouched portion of Annabel's rubbery cheesecake had been cleared away, Tess appeared at the podium and began the award portion of the evening. Max checked the program and noted that theirs would be the sixth and final public service category announced. In a show of support, he took Annabel's hand in his, although he didn't know how long he could stand it. Her grip cut off more of his circulation with each announcement. At this rate, by the time their turn came, she'd be crushing bones.

His pulse accelerated more when he thought about Annabel's name being announced as the winner than it did thinking of his own. Some network hotshot had called him again that day to hint that winning the award would put the job in the bag for him, but he might be able to talk his way into the network position without it, if necessary. Annabel's chance to continue doing the work she loved was in real jeopardy.

Finally, Nick Clooney, George's dad, politician, former news anchor, and local celebrity, took the stage to announce their category, Best Public Service/Media Award. As he read the list of nominees, Annabel's face brightened and her smile stretched. Max's heart convulsed with pride and anxiety for her, and he missed hearing his own name when Nick read it.

Winning the award didn't mean nearly as much to him as he had thought. Not nearly as much as it would mean to Annabel. At the last moment—and contrary to every ambitious and competitive bone in his body—he almost hoped she would win instead of him.

"And the winner is—" Nick paused for the usual fumbling of the envelope and dramatic pause before proclaiming, "*Art for Art's Sake*, Heartfelt Productions, Lynn Dorey, producer."

*Damn.* Applause burst around them, and Max joined in. No

point in looking like a poor loser when the camera panned his face for a reaction. He smiled and nodded like he'd known it all along, but his gaze quickly turned to Annabel. Her taut expression revealed her pain, even though she clapped and smiled politely.

"Lynn Dorey," he said to her with a dismissive shrug. She nodded, and then he repeated it to their bosses as if they hadn't heard. "Lynn Dorey."

"Tough luck, kiddo." Howard tipped her a salute with his glass of scotch before knocking back a healthy slug.

"Better luck next time, dear." His wife adjusted the rows of diamond bracelets on her wrist.

"Yours was a damn fine piece," Charley said to Max. "These competitions are a crapshoot."

"Oh, I wanted it to be one of you two." Shawntel pouted as she kissed Max on the cheek. "You're still the best in my book."

The woman at the podium made her acceptance speech, gracious, witty, generous in her praise of the other nominees. *Blah, blah, blah.* She came and went, then Tess returned to the spotlight.

And Annabel sat frozen beside him, fragile enough to crack like ice under pressure. Amazing that he knew her well enough now to know she donned the Ice Princess persona when she cared too much to let her real feelings show.

Stroking his fingers along her arm while she battled her emotions, he waited to grab an opportunity for them to leave without making a scene. Willing to do almost anything to cheer her up, he could only think of one thing.

He leaned over and whispered in her ear, "Come on, darlin'. We're outta here."

The limo glided up to the curb on command. At least some things happened as expected. Draping her sparkly shawl around her shoulders, Annabel huddled in on herself. Max hustled her through the drizzling rain and into the backseat of the car.

As the car made its way out of downtown, she remained numb inside. He undid his tie and loosened the button on his collar before perusing the bottles in the mini-bar. The level of concern he angled her way in a series of side glances failed to penetrate her sense of loss. He made a couple of encouraging remarks, but she didn't have the heart to respond.

She shouldn't be so disappointed. It wasn't that important. What was one little local media award, more or less? Max sure didn't seem concerned about losing, or else he hid it better behind his on-camera face than she did.

Lynn Dorey had produced a fine piece.

Life moved on.

No big deal.

Except that she wanted to win.

She had said that winning the award would prove to Howard her ability to produce award-winning work. That winning the award would compel him to allow her to work on projects worthy of her talent. But that wasn't it.

Either he would allow her to produce or he wouldn't. He should be aware of her talents by this time, award or no award. She could stand up to him and demand her chance. She could go elsewhere to do the work she wanted to do.

What she had really wanted… needed… *craved*, in fact, was the acknowledgment that she was the very best at what she did. Better than the infamous Max Williams. Better than the accomplished Lynn Dorey. Better than everyone.

Not a very magnanimous reason for wanting to win a public service award, shame forced her to admit, but the admission needed to be faced.

Failure pressed in on her, making her feel weak and diminished. Alone and cold. Very, very cold, like the Ice Princess Max always called her.

She dabbed tears from the corners of her eyes. Max took her hand and closed her fingers around a glass of champagne. She put the glass in a holder and warmed a bit only when Max reclaimed her hand, cradling it in his.

"You're supposed to drink that. I was going to propose a toast. Something clever about being too classy to be losers."

"Not now, please." Her stiff lips refused to smile any longer. She shivered, watching the rain sheet the window.

"You're freezing." He scooted closer and slid an arm around her shoulders. "We need brandy, or scotch, not champagne." He stretched his other arm toward the mini-bar again.

"No, I just want to go home." She cuddled closer to his warmth.

"Do you have brandy at your house?" His breath washed across her cheek. The hair on the back of her neck stood up.

Did she have brandy? Probably not. She shook her head. Max tapped on the glass and gave the driver an address.

"Where are we going?" Her teeth chattered around the question.

"My place." He wrapped his other arm around her and gathered her to him. His hands slid under her shawl, moving over her arms, back, neck, and shoulders, soothing and healing.

If she weren't so cold, so frozen, she'd move away. But for now, she needed all the heat he could give her. "No, just take me home."

His fixed gaze drilled into her with the precision of a laser. It penetrated the cold sense of failure down to her very bones, to the place that terrified her.

"Fine." He tapped on the glass to issue new directions.

Through the rain-streaked windows, she saw the lights ablaze inside her house, offering a false sense of welcome. Carly was out for the night, but the girl never remembered to turn off the lights when she left. Annabel dreaded going inside and huddling alone with her disappointment.

A pair of warm pajamas and a cup of cappuccino might comfort her. Or a less-sophisticated pleasure, like hot cocoa. Double chocolate with extra marshmallows. She could thaw out her frozen brain, indulge in a brief pity party, and maybe allow herself a few tears as she went to sleep. Then she'd get up and face the morning with a new perspective. She'd think about the future then.

Max bundled her through the rain and onto the covered porch. He lowered the umbrella provided by Eduardo and took the keys from her hand when she fumbled with the lock.

"You sure you're all right?" Max asked. "I hate to leave you here alone." He turned Annabel toward him and tilted her face toward the light.

"I'm fine." The lie almost stuck in her throat. If she weren't fine now, she would be by tomorrow. She'd had plenty of practice getting through life's kicks in the teeth on her own.

He shook his head, disbelieving. His dark eyes locked with hers, rimmed with sympathy and kindness, but also questioning and persuasive. She shivered again.

With his warm hands on her bare shoulders, steam skittered

across her skin. He pulled her forward inch by slow inch. His head slanted to one side, and then his lips covered hers. Warmth, glorious warmth shot through her everywhere their bodies met, blocking out the chill of her defeat.

Forget hot chocolate. Marshmallows be damned. Max made her forget her loss better than an entire vat of Swiss Miss. The thought of him leaving made her ache with longing. She wrapped herself around him and pressed into him, desperate for comfort.

When she parted her lips and his tongue swept inside, he gave a hungry growl, spreading his incredible warmth inside her. One kiss led to another. Places she'd forgotten about began to tingle.

His mouth grazed her neck in a tantalizing trail. Hot breath caressed her flesh. Hands skimmed her breasts. The starched pleats on his shirt brushed her taut nipples. Her shivers no longer emanated from the numbing cold, but from the heat of longing.

The flash of lights from a car passing her house jerked her back to reality. She shifted her mouth away from his with a gasp. As much as she wanted him and craved the oblivion he offered, she couldn't do this.

Not on her front doorstep.

"Let's go in," he suggested, reading her mind.

Her moment's hesitation provided him with the opportunity to back her through the doorway into the foyer. He closed the door behind him.

"We shouldn't do this." She planted her hands on the solid wall of his chest, gesturing in the general direction of her driveway and the waiting limo. "We *can't* do this. What will Eduardo think?"

"Eduardo will be thrilled." He rubbed his palms along her bare back, then pulled her close. "He gets paid by the hour."

Annabel's curiosity spiked along with her desire as his fingers searched for the fastening on her dress. "How long will it take?"

He gave her a pure-Max smile. One that sent her sexual appetite zinging off the gotta-have-it scale. "How long have you got?"

"I've got all night." She startled herself, first, with the thought, and then, with the realization. *They were going to do this.*

*Sex with Max was going to happen.* No more stalling. No more excuses. She took a deep breath and plunged ahead. "Let's make Eduardo rich."

# Chapter Nine

"All night, huh?" Max smiled widely. "You got it, babe." The heat in his eyes guaranteed the promise as he removed her sparkly wrap and tossed it aside. His hands skimmed her bare back, moved down her sides, then to the front of the diaphanous material. "It might take all night to figure out how to get you out of this thing."

"Let me help." Annabel guided him to the zipper on the side of the dress. She reached up to undo the magic hook that held the two straps together at the nape of her neck.

Before the material fell away and revealed her bare breasts, Max covered her hands with his, stopping her. "If you're not into exhibitionism, the foyer's better than the front porch, but do you really want to do this here?" He pressed his hips against hers, indicating the hard ridge of his erection. "I'm game, but you might want some place more comfortable."

A bit of her chill returned with his practical suggestion, but his fingers massaged small circles along her back and ignited heated tingling along her spine that melted hesitation away. She'd love to be the kind of sensual woman who enjoyed having sex any time, any place, but she'd never been that woman before. For this first time in such a long time, she'd probably enjoy it more somewhere else.

Someplace where the vast difference in their levels of experience would be less apparent.

Somewhere safe.

Definitely somewhere dark.

"Upstairs?" she suggested.

At his quick nod, she leaned in for a taste of his beautifully decadent mouth. Definitely better than hot chocolate. Or a hot fudge sundae. Or a freaking mountain of chocolate. One nip led to two. She deepened the kiss with a stroke of her tongue. His lips parted to welcome her inside.

Her hips arched against him, pressing into his rock-hard cock. His hands slipped inside her dress, cupped her breasts, and held their weight in his palms. She let out a long breath that had lodged itself somewhere around her ribcage. When his thumbs brushed across her nipples, she moaned. So did he.

An encouraging flutter frisked around inside her stomach at the intensity of his response. Knowing she had the ability to arouse him so quickly and forcefully ignited her confidence.

"We have *got* to get you out of this dress." His voice was ragged with frustration.

"Upstairs." She intended to be cloaked in shadow before shedding her clothing.

Holding onto her hips, he backed her toward the steps. She reached up to brush her fingers through the soft, thick hair at his temple. He stopped short, and she stumbled. When he opened his mouth to speak, she kissed him instead.

What was it about his mouth that she found so irresistible? The firm, wide shape? The full lips or beautiful teeth? Had she ever been so fascinated with any other mouth? God, she didn't think so.

His hands slipped inside the front of her dress again, caressing her breasts. He flashed his sexiest, most photogenic smile. "Thank God, I was right."

"About what? That I'm not very… very…"

"Very what?"

"You know. Not very big." She dropped her forehead to his chest so she didn't have to look at him. "Voluptuous."

"You're plenty big. If you weren't, why would I have been wondering all through dinner what you did or didn't have on under here? That was the only thing that kept me awake through some of those speeches."

A bubble of laughter escaped her, delighted by the idea of holding his attention smack dab in the middle of some of Cincinnati's most beautiful women.

"Let me see you," he said, his voice low and coaxing.

The laughter stuck in her throat as he returned her hands to the hooks that held the halter in place. The shimmery material dropped away. His breath caught as he admired her naked flesh.

"Let me see *you*." The daring words shocked her, but she was determined not to be the only nearly-naked person in her foyer.

She removed his dangling necktie and started on his shirt studs. Every part of him she uncovered exceeded her sexual fantasies. Solid muscles, lean and taut. Crisp chest hair. Just as she got to the hardest, flattest stomach she'd ever fantasized about touching, his vest interrupted her journey.

Sliding her arms around him, she unhooked it in the back. The maneuver brought her breasts firmly against the inflexible wall of his naked chest.

She rubbed against him like a cat, savoring the contrasting textures of his pleated shirt and crinkly hair on her hyper-sensitive skin. Dipping her head, she took a deep whiff of his scent—spicy cologne, starched cotton, and fresh, clean male. He looked and smelled so delicious she wanted to take a bite out of him. Her mouth settled for a nibble at the appealing bend between his shoulder and neck.

"Come on, babe." He led her another few steps toward the stairs, but the yards of material swirled around their feet, tangled around them, and got in the way of walking and touching.

Frustrated, Annabel thrust the dress below her hips. She smiled as it slithered to the floor. Boldly, she stepped out of it and kicked it aside.

Then she froze behind years of wallflower insecurity.

Only his hands on hers prevented her from covering the exposed areas. His gaze moved up and down her body once, visually caressing every inch, then he made the trip a second time, his face a study in amazement.

"What?" A prolonged moment of silence hung in the air while Annabel considered the nearest place to hide.

"You're beautiful. Perfect." His hand trailed appreciatively along her side, from her breast to her hip. He groaned again and shook his head. "To think this is what you've been hiding, and I didn't know." He bent to let his mouth follow the path his hand had taken. "I'm usually a better judge than that."

Clad only in a wisp of panties, sheer stockings and the sexiest little shoes she'd ever worn, Annabel felt a blush migrate from her forehead to her toes. She opened her mouth to refute the compliment, but he tapped a finger against her lips.

"Everything about you is beautiful. Don't argue. Just say thank you."

Reading the admiration in his eyes, she wanted to let herself believe him. "Th-thank you."

"Promise you'll never disguise yourself in nun's clothes again." His lips grazed hers. "Promise me that."

She shoved his jacket and shirt aside. Her hands drifted over the sculpted planes, from abs and pecs to biceps, shoulders and back. With so much to explore, her fingers shook as she unfastened his pants.

"Promise me." His whispered breath rasped across her skin, setting off a barrage of goose bumps.

"I promise." With every delicious detail of his magnificent body revealed in front of her, ready, willing and eager for her explorations, she couldn't remember what promise he demanded from her. She would have assured him of anything in that moment when she touched his upright cock for the first time. Big, thick, hard. Way beyond her expectations.

Gathering her close, he sighed with relief as if her response made a difference to him. "I'm going to touch you and taste you all over. Starting now."

"I want that, too. To touch you, taste you." Did she dare do any of that? Would he want her to? Barely able to speak any longer, she gestured vaguely up the stairs. "Bedroom.'

Shaking his head, he pulled her down with him. "Next time."

As they moved in perfect syncopation through the same erotic dance, he aroused her to dizzying hunger, teasing her sexual appetite with rare and exotic treats. Lost in the pooling warmth of desire, she tried to keep up, to participate and reciprocate, but he was way out of her league. Sometimes, she was so overwhelmed with sensations, it was all she could do to remember to breathe. She couldn't get enough of him, certainly not in an hour.

Or even a night.

Not when he licked his way down her body. Not when he slipped his fingers through her slick folds. Not when he lifted and seated her across his hips, sliding deep inside her, stretching, filling, and bringing her home. Sweet, never-before-known sensations swamped her as he thrust into her, over and over, surrounding her with the feel, taste, and smell of him.

*Max!* With crystal-sharp clarity, she looked deep into his eyes and matched him move for move.

She rode the unbelievable sensations higher and higher, unable to stop, almost unable to breathe. As she hovered on the brink of exquisite, almost unbearable pleasure, he leaned back and put a hand to her chin, fixing her gaze with a question in his.

"Yes, please. Now." Her eyelids fluttered. "You come, too."

His final thrust took her over the edge. He followed her with a triumphant shout that made her smile.

After a few minutes, she stretched out full-length against him, fully aware of the nakedness of his body beneath hers. Resting against him should have been about as comfortable as snuggling a slab of marble, but somehow, it suited her.

Slowly, she came to realize the awkwardness of her position, not just emotionally or socially awkward, but physically awkward as well. She raised her head to determine the problem. She seemed to be... diagonal.

They'd made it as far as the stairs. She eased herself away, perching on the step beside him. "Oh, God. You are awesome good."

Max lay stretched with his feet grazing the floor and his shoulders about six steps up. He turned his head toward her and gave a cocky grin at the words she hadn't intended to say out loud.

Suddenly, the realization of what they'd done, where they'd done it, and all his gorgeous nudity was too much to consider in one gulp. She wanted to sprint upstairs to hide, but imagined the view that would provide. Instead, she slid into a boneless puddle onto the foyer's hard ceramic tile floor.

Nonchalantly—as if she entertained naked men in her foyer every day—she gathered her hair on top of her head, but she couldn't decide where to fix her eyes. His ankles got most of her attention. They were nice ankles. Sturdy. Neutral.

She felt his gaze on her, glanced up as far as his knees, chickened out and looked away. "If it's not too indelicate to mention such a thing, I'm sweating." The air had turned into a sauna around them.

She winced. *Charming.* Probably the most charming thing anyone had ever said to him during afterglow.

"At least you're not cold anymore." Beside her, he sat up and planted his elbows on his knees. He stroked his palm over her hair and sifted a few of the curly strands through his fingers, sensual and comforting.

She was transfixed by the tattoo the movement revealed. A lightning bolt ran along his left side from beneath his armpit to his hip. *Dear Lord.* How had she missed that before? She reached out, wanting to touch it, but pulled her hand back.

"You're embarrassed," he said, "and you shouldn't be."

She ducked her head again, even more chagrined to know he read her so easily. "Aren't you?"

"A little." He reached out and tilted her chin up. When she gathered the courage to look at him, he rewarded her with an intimate smile—equally sexy and endearing, damn him. "That wasn't my best effort."

"What?"

"I can do a lot better."

She found his comment a little intriguing and a little hurtful. *How* much better could he be? And what about *her* was so lacking that it caused him to perform at less than his best? "Why didn't you?"

He shrugged. "I hate to admit it, but I got distracted."

"By what?" She was ready to toss him out on his bare, and oh, so fabulous butt if his mind had been on some mundane and unrelated topic instead of his performance.

"By you." He reached for her.

If a heart could melt, hers did.

He was the most surprising man she'd ever known—not that she'd known that many. Every day of the past week, she'd learned something new about him. And today, he'd taught her something new about herself. She was as susceptible to Max Williams' charms as every other woman in the free world.

She didn't want to think about it.

She didn't want to think about *anything*.

Tomorrow, she'd deal with the fallout. Tonight, she'd take what she could get.

"By me?" She settled deliciously into his lap.

"By your sexy body, your sensuality, your sweetness, and your surprising assertiveness. Dynamite combination. Everything about you was so much more than I expected. You astounded me." He nuzzled her neck and licked her ear, catapulting her senses into another round of sexual frolicking. "Want me to make it up to you?"

"I might be willing to give you a second chance." She did her best to sound reluctant, when she was already plotting the things she wanted to do to him. "But this time we really should go upstairs."

"You're on." He laughed, gathered her close, grabbed his pants from the stair rail, and then surged to his feet. "The stairs *might* have been another thing that distracted me."

Yep, *that* was better. Max settled Annabel at his side an hour or so later. Not that the first time hadn't been fantastic, but it had been fast and furious and he hadn't taken enough time to make Annabel feel she was everything he wanted in a woman.

But this time, the second time had been right up there with his best.

Perfect timing. Stimulation, satisfaction, quantity and quality… all perfect. Better than perfect. They might have to do it again before he figured out what made it so special. As soon as humanly possible. If he hadn't been totally drained of all energy, he'd smile at the prospect.

He summoned the strength to draw Annabel closer. While he waited to rebound, he wanted to keep her near enough to feel and smell and touch. She was just the right height to pillow her head on his shoulder and lie next to him without any awkward bumping elbows, knees, or shins.

He hoped she wouldn't want to talk but he supposed that was asking too much. Women always wanted to talk, and not about pleasure, fantasies, technique or staying power, but about *meaning* and *feelings*. As if doing what felt good had to mean something more than that. And maybe it did. Not that he was ready to consider giving up his freedom for a woman. Not like his old man had. Not ready to be left with a trio of hungry brats and no one to warm his bed at night.

Mr. Free and Easy. That was Max. Especially now, when he was about to sign a fan-damn-frigging-tastic deal and achieve a major career goal.

And if someone did eventually make him want to give up on that, did compel him to stick around, it wouldn't be for a long, long time, and it wouldn't be Annabel Morgan.

No matter how warm and wild she'd been when he was inside her wet heat. No matter how perfectly she fit into his arms.

He knew they weren't destined to be together long-term. She didn't want that and neither did he. If something about that thought made him irritable, he didn't stop to examine it. She'd made it clear from the get-go that she didn't think they'd ever be anything more than casual friends.

Of course, he doubted if she'd ever pictured him in her bed either, and here he was.

His spirits lifted a notch until another unwelcome thought punctured his optimism. Her busy little brain was already probably thinking up a hundred good reasons to kick him out of her bed right now. But he hoped not.

The sparks that flared between them hadn't even come close to burning themselves out yet. Not by a long shot.

Looking down at Annabel, he saw that she looked— something. Something he couldn't put his finger on. Tense? Thoughtful? Distant?

"How do you feel—" She paused to raise up on her elbow and lean her head against her hand.

*Ah ha! Here it comes!* That's what they always wanted to know.

"—about not winning the award?"

*Where had that come from?* "A little bummed, I guess." And a little pissed to know that he hadn't held her attention for more than five minutes past her mind-blowing climax. Her *second* one! Had she been thinking about the damned award the whole time they'd been mak—having sex?

She smoothed his hair off his forehead in a comforting gesture, but he pulled away. He couldn't believe she thought he needed comfort. He had been comforting *her*, and now, she tried turning the tables on him!

"I thought if *I* didn't win the award, *you* would." Her fingers trailed tentatively across his shoulder.

"I guess I just didn't sleep with the right person," Max joked, although all he really wanted to do was roll her onto her back and make her shout down the roof again. He still couldn't believe Annabel was such a screamer.

"Is that how she did it?" Annabel asked, eyebrows raised in shock.

Just because she tested his control beyond endurance and made his blood pound, he sometimes forgot what an innocent she really was, until she said something that naive.

"How else would you explain it?"

She pushed her hair off her forehead, raising her arm and diverting his attention to where the sheet slipped down to her waist.

"Talent?" she suggested, tugging the sheet back into place. "Topical subject matter? The backing of her production company?"

"We had all that, too."

She cocked her head to the side and studied him in a way that was so knowing and so wise that it made him want to grab his pants and run. "*Would* you have slept with someone just to win?"

His eyes crinkled into a smile as he tightened his arm around her. "Only you."

"You seem to be taking it pretty well."

"What? Sleeping with you?"

"No, losing."

Why did they have to talk about this now? If he wanted to bare his soul, he'd have gone to bed with the station's sexy lady shrink who'd been sending him some pretty strong do-me signals for the past few months. "I won't be if you keep repeating the L-word like that."

"Seriously."

Damn, he hated hearing that word, especially in a beautiful woman's bed. "I wanted to win the award to brush up my image for a network job. Just being nominated might have done the trick, but I'll know soon enough."

Her hand on his chest stilled, interrupting the erotic pattern she'd been tracing. "Is the job in New York or LA?"

"New York. Didn't I tell you?" He tried hard to sound casual, knowing he had hinted about it at best. Still it wasn't like they were joined at the hip—not usually anyway. And no contract had been signed. "Investigative journalist for a national program. I might still do some on-camera work, but mostly I'd be developing and investigating the stories."

"What a great opportunity." Her enthusiasm rang a bit forced. "When will you know?"

"Soon. My agent's hammering out the deal now."

"Well, congratulations." She leaned over and gave him a stiff-lipped kiss, more maiden aunt than hot new lover. "No wonder you weren't as concerned about winning the award as I was."

"Howard will still let you do what you want now, won't he?"

"Oh, sure," she said too quickly, not meeting his eyes.

Her future was not his concern. But still. "What will you do if he doesn't?"

"Something else." She shrugged, pretending indifference. Worst liar Max had even known. "Meanwhile, do you know what I'd like?"

"I hope so." He started easing the sheet from her grip. Even though the mood for romance had been strangled out of him about ten minutes ago, he might be able to revive it with the right incentive.

"I'm hungry," she announced, tracing his tattoo down his side.

"Hey, me, too, babe." He reached for her. She stopped him with his mouth a half-inch from her breast.

"For *food.*"

"No wonder." He sighed, disappointed, but understanding. "You hardly ate any of the rubber chicken at the dinner."

She tossed the covers back and hopped out of bed. "Give me a minute, and I'll make you an omelet."

Her bare ass disappeared into the bathroom.

꙳

*Idiot!* Annabel turned the shower on full blast. *Of course, his plans don't include me.* Tonight was nothing more than two people coming together on a night of mutual need. If he turned out to be funny and personable, sweet and gentle, it was because he'd had a lot of practice at moments like these.

She'd wanted to put some zip and zing into her life, and now she knew—too much zing took the zip right out of her. Still, it had been a night to remember. She intended to put on her happiest face for whatever time they had left. He'd said she could have all night. That meant they had about three or four more hours. She'd make the most of them.

After she stepped out of the shower and dried off, she reached for her flannel robe. It zipped down the front, had a hood, and made her look more like a linebacker than a femme fatale. Definitely not sexy enough for Max. She returned the robe to its hook.

She went into the bedroom to grab something with a little more pizazz from her dresser. Max blessedly had his back turned, bent over putting on his trousers. She paused to enjoy the view until the outcome of the action registered. Putting on his pants!

"Are you leaving?" She clapped her hand over her mouth as soon as the words were out.

He turned and looked at her. First, like he was appalled by her question. Then, like she was nuts. And finally, like she was naked. She liked the third look the best.

"No, we're going downstairs." He pulled another condom from his pocket. "And being a former Boy Scout—always prepared—I thought we might need this."

"Oh, thank heavens! You have another one." She went over and put her arms around his neck, brushing lots of bare skin against him. He sucked in his stomach as all his muscles turned to granite. Encouraged, she let her hands slide over the contours of his back.

"Last one." He cupped her bottom and pressed his erection into her. "We can use it now or later. Your choice." His kiss encouraged *now*.

She wanted him again, already. And incredibly, he seemed to be hers for the taking. For the moment. Unused to the instant gratification of any of her desires, let alone sexual ones, she hesitated. She knew the value of waiting for what she wanted. "If we use it now, there won't be any later?"

"Well, we'd have to improvise. But I have some ideas about that." He knelt in front of her and kissed the heart-shaped birthmark on her hip.

"Improvisation is good." She clutched his head, unsure whether she wanted to pull him to her or push him away. His mouth caressing her intimately was a much-anticipated fantasy. One that had kept her awake for several nights and was totally outside her limited experience.

"Sometimes, improvisation is the best." He kissed a path across her stomach and dipped his tongue into her navel.

She trembled. *Too much!* Definitely too much. But she wanted what was coming next. She feared it. She doubted if she could live without it. Still... She made a half-hearted attempt to delay. "But anticipation is good, too."

"Oh, yeah," he agreed. "Love anticipation." He nestled his face against the triangle of curls and let his tongue tease her slick flesh. "But I love the taste of you more."

His mouth took her then and caressed her at the exact spot

where every sensation pooled. She didn't know she could *feel* this much. *It's too much. Too much.* The refrain repeated in her head with the rhythm of his tongue against her until too much was not nearly enough.

She sucked great gulps of air into her lungs as the pressure built and her fists tightened in his hair. As his tongue rasped over her faster and faster, her climax came closer and closer. She felt hot all over and dizzy, and so, *so* good. She tensed and arched her hips against him, shouting her release as her orgasm slammed into her, overwhelming and compacting all other sensations into one powerful, defining focus. She surfed the wave of the moment, longing for it to last forever.

Her knees had never failed her before, but now, they buckled. Only her grip on his muscular shoulders kept her from crumbling into a heap. Light-headed, she eased to the floor in front of him, thighs straddling thighs, forehead touching forehead. Shaken, she couldn't speak. If he made a wisecrack, she'd smack him.

He leaned back a fraction and looked at her, his eyes filled with wonder. His fingers went to her cheeks, touching the moisture she hadn't realized was there. "Hey, you're not supposed to cry. I wanted to make you feel good."

"Good is such an inadequate word." She closed her eyes and dropped her head onto his shoulder. "That far exceeded good. Thank you."

Encircling her in his arms, he rocked her back and forth while she fought to control her unruly emotions.

"You're—I never—Oh, my." She paused to catch her breath. "*That* was incredible."

"Have you never done *that* before?"

Reduced to a physical and emotional puddle, she could only shake her head.

"Why not? You obviously enjoyed it."

Why not, indeed? It seemed disrespectful to think of her husband and compare him unfavorably. "My husband was older. Very dignified, very reserved."

"Very boring."

"Not boring," The disloyal thought shamed her. "He just wasn't as interested or comfortable with sex as you are."

"Was he gay?"

"No!"

"Then there's no excuse."

She remembered the nights Carl came to bed, pajama-clad. He'd reach for her and enter her so silently, so distantly. They'd never shared this kind of pleasure in their intimacy. Even though it had been less than fulfilling for her, she'd thought she might be the one who was lacking. She never realized how much laughter and emotion could be shared in the moment. "I don't think he would have enjoyed it."

"He should have." The color of Max's dark eyes deepened. "You're incredible, you know. You should be with someone who appreciates you."

She covered her ears with her hands. "Don't say anything more about him."

"Sorry. You're right. It's not my place to talk about the things your husband did or didn't do for you." Max cupped her cheeks in his palms, rubbing her cheeks with his thumbs. "But don't waste any more of your life limited by someone else's boundaries, okay?"

He looked so serious, so adorable with his gaze locked on hers. He'd opened doors to sensual thresholds she'd only read about. Drawn to him on emotional levels he wouldn't welcome, she opened her mouth to express feelings he wouldn't want to hear. As if reading her mind, he touched his fingers to her lips and shook his head.

She swallowed and formed the most difficult words of the night. Words that just might be necessary to her self-preservation. "Maybe you should go."

"Go?" His eyebrows shot up. "No way, lady. I promised you all night, and you promised me an omelet."

An omelet. That put things into perspective.

If he could be nonchalant, so could she.

Even if it killed her.

# Chapter Ten

Relieved to escape getting the boot, Max peered out of the blinds in Annabel's bedroom. The limo remained in the driveway. While he and Annabel had screwed one another upside down and sideways, the persistent drizzle had escalated into an all-out storm, complete with window-rattling thunder and lightning.

Annabel slipped into some purple shorts and a silky top that were too revealing to be anything other than underwear, but way too delicious to be covered up by regular clothes. With an intimate smile, she took his hand and led him downstairs.

"Do you know who makes the best Denver omelet in Cincinnati?" They arrived for his first visit to her kitchen. Nice, efficient, tidy. Just as he expected, the counters gleamed. Not even a dirty fork lurked in the sink. He'd see about changing that.

"Duffy's on the River?"

"No, Ms. Smarty Pants." He slipped his fingers into the waist of her little shorts and snapped the elastic. "I do."

"Oh, really? Then wash your hands and get to work." She retrieved an armload of ingredients from the refrigerator, laying them out precisely on the counter. "I'll make the bacon and toast."

"And coffee. We have to have coffee."

Pointing to the kettle, she wrinkled her nose. "Not tea?"

He scoffed. "Tea's for wimps. If we're going to stay busy all night, we need high-octane caffeine."

"Good point." She reached into the pantry for K-cups.

Her skimpy top rode up her back, exposing a flash of smooth skin. He gravitated forward to wrap his arms around her waist. She deftly avoided him and shoved the chopping board and a knife into his hands.

He attacked a green pepper with his usual fervor. He didn't cook often, but when he did, he put a lot of energy into it. After several strips of green pepper sailed across the chopping block and onto the floor, Annabel crossed her arms and pretended to glare at him.

"What?" He tossed an onion over his shoulder and caught it behind his back. "You've never seen anyone cook before?"

"Not with such abandon." She shoved a bowl his way. "Here. You break the eggs. I'll finish chopping. It worries me to see you wielding a sharp object."

Chewing on her bottom lip, she proceeded to lay strips of peppers side by side and cut them into uniform squares. Next, he figured she'd measure them with a slide rule.

Planning to wow her with his proudest kitchen accomplishment, he picked up an egg in each hand, tapped both against the side of the bowl, and then cracked them open at the same time. The egg-innards slid into the bowl. He deftly pitched the shells into the trash with a basketball hook shot. He looked up to see if she'd caught his grandstanding.

She had. Pushing him aside, she chased a minuscule shell fragment around the bowl with a spoon. "I see you like your omelets crunchy."

"You don't worry about a few eggshells, do you?" He trapped the speck beneath a fingertip and flicked it aside. "A little roughage is good for you."

"Uh huh." She pursed her lips together, obviously trying to keep herself from either scolding him or laughing. He wondered which one.

She followed along behind him after that, taking over every task he started, from whisking the eggs to adding the splash of hot sauce. When he prepared to flip the omelets without benefit of a spatula, she took the pan away from him. "I'll do it. You go butter the toast."

"You know what your problem is?" he asked as they sat down to eat. "You're a control freak with no sense of adventure."

"Really?" She looked around at the chaos he'd made of her formerly spotless kitchen. "And you're a disaster waiting to happen."

"I might be messy, but I'm fun."

"True." She hid a yawn behind her hand.

"Sleepy?"

"A little. I'm not used to staying up all night, are you?"

"It happens." Just the night before he'd stayed up until

dawn on a pointless stakeout. But even that was more productive than most of his all-nighters. "Can you sleep late tomorrow?"

She frowned at the clock on the wall. "It's almost two A.M. So, tomorrow is already today, and I have a yoga class at nine." She rubbed her eyes with her knuckles. "I might have to skip that. What are your plans?"

"I'm running in a charity race at eight. What about in the afternoon?"

"Attending a tea at The Conservatory. Are you riding with the motorcycle club?"

"Not until Sunday. Tomorrow afternoon I have tickets to see the Reds."

"Can you rest after that?"

Rest on a Saturday night? Not until he was dead. "Nah, it's my poker night. Will you be turning in early?"

"Probably, but first, I have to go visit my aunt in the hospital."

*Man, we really don't have anything in common. Too bad.* Things had gone so well between them tonight. He'd like to spend more time with her, but didn't have to be hit over the head to see that their schedules and interests didn't coincide anyplace but in bed. That might be enough for him, but he had a feeling she'd want more.

And he was surprised to note, he kind of wanted more, too.

She popped a piece of bacon into her mouth and followed it with her last bite of egg. Holding her coffee cup in one hand, she rested her chin on the heel of the other. She beamed at him, and the warmth of her smile caressed him from across the table. And his immediate physical reaction didn't have a thing to do with the cleavage peeking at him over the plunge of her purple silk tank.

Realizing it had been too long since he'd touched her, he pushed his chair back, prepared to change that.

"You *do* make the best omelet in Cincinnati."

"Why, thank you, ma'am." Moving to stand behind her, he adopted an exaggerated aw-shucks stance. "But you did all the work."

She leaned her head back and smiled at him upside down. "I'd say we did it together. We made a good team."

He pressed a kiss to her soft lips. She tasted of coffee and strawberry jam, and he let his mouth linger. Without breaking contact, he pivoted to kneel beside her. She enclosed him in her sweet-smelling embrace.

"Know what we should do now?" His voice was a whisper as his lips moved on hers.

"Clean the kitchen?"

"Sure, let's do that." He moved to cup her breasts, feeling the weight in his palms. "Later."

She sighed with pleasure as he teased first one and then the other with his mouth, dampening the thin material. With his tongue coaxing her nipples to hard points, his hands moved a slow path from ribs to hip to inner thigh. He felt her twitch with impatience, but he intended to prolong the game of stimulation indefinitely.

Each time they'd been physical, he'd given her something different.

This time, he wanted her to have a total out-of-body experience. From nibbling her earlobes to her toes, he didn't want her to miss a thing. He fully intended to linger... *everywhere.*

"Ma-ax?" Her voice came out a throaty croak.

"Hmmm?" He nuzzled the valley between her breasts.

"Please."

"Please what, darlin'?"

"Just do it."

"Anna-honey," he drawled over a slow smile, "this isn't a sixty-second sneaker commercial. We've got all night, remember?"

He continued his slow exploration until she groaned with frustration. Finally, when he allowed himself to rake the material aside with his teeth and take the inviting peak into his mouth, he realized he'd pushed her too far. She reached down and touched his erection, her hand trailing the length of the hard heat that sat up and begged for her attention. With each tentative stroke, his desire intensified.

Tired of waiting for him to give her what she wanted, she put her other hand between her legs and rubbed her own sweet spot. He about lost control. Damn it, watching sweet, almost inexperienced Annabel touch herself was about the hottest thing he'd ever seen.

He reached out and pushed the dishes aside. Putting his hands around her waist, he lifted her from the chair to the tabletop.

His pulse hammered in his head.

His ears began to buzz.

He paused for a second to get a grip, but it was impossible not to enjoy the delectable picture she made laid back across the table, with her hand inside her purple panties, fingering herself. Sweet Jesus. He broke out in a sweat.

The buzz persisted as he slid the panties down her legs.

He shook his head and it persisted still. "Well, hell. It's my phone." He reached into his trouser pocket and pulled out the phone and condom. He checked the text and groaned. He'd half expected this message all week, so of course this is when it would come, just when Annabel was about to come, too. He placed the rubber in the palm of Annabel's free hand and closed her fingers around it. "Hold onto this and don't stop what you're doing. I'll be right back."

Not wanting her to overhear this conversation, he hit Mercer's number and moved painfully into the foyer.

"Damn it," he growled into the phone. "Does it have to be now?"

"Nope." The voice grated against his ear like gravel in a cement mixer. "If you don't want the proof you need..."

"Are you sure this time?" Max demanded. "Or will it be another waste of time like before?"

"Hey, these guys aren't the bus company. They don't print a schedule. The truck is pulling up to the warehouse now. Get your ass over here if you want to get pictures."

"I'll be there in ten."

"I'll need my money."

Max cursed again. "You'll get it when I've got my story."

Despite his frustration with the timing, his pulse kicked up at the thought of finally exposing these assholes. He wanted to bust these guys. The exposure would do more for his career opportunities than winning some award. He took a second to call Roger to tell him where to meet him downtown.

After making the necessary arrangements, Max adjusted the semi-hard ridge pressing against his fly and gathered the rest of his clothes. He shrugged into his shirt and jacket. With only a cursory look around, he couldn't find the bowtie or one of his socks. He grabbed the stupid vest and stuffed it into his pocket.

A filmy stocking curled like a gossamer ribbon around one

of his shoes. He picked up the intimate item and stroked the silky texture through his fingers. On a whim, he pocketed the personal memento, too.

Sliding his feet into his shoes, he eyed the front door. In the interest of time, he considered the advantages of taking off without a word, but that seemed too low, even for him.

Besides, this was Annabel. She deserved better. He knew if he left her now in such a position and without explanation, he'd never see her again. Of course, it was possible he'd never see her again anyway, even if he did try to explain. That thought sent him rushing back to her.

In the kitchen, he found her rinsing dishes in the sink. The yardstick rigidity of her spine told him she already understood their night was over. Just as well. If she'd still been spread across the table like a porno all-you-can-eat buffet, he probably would have dived right back in.

"I'm sorry." From behind her, he slipped his arms around her waist and kissed the side of her neck, inhaling deeply to carry her scent away with him. "I have to go."

"I figured."

"It's work."

"I understand." Her tone didn't match her words. She said she understood, but her tone said she'd carry a grudge all the same. She turned inside the circle of his arms to face him. "Is it Mercer?"

He donned his best poker face. "Mercer, who?"

"Ed Mercer, the guy you met the other day on the poker run. Works at City Hall."

He looked at her sharply. "How do you know that?"

She rocked back on her heels and looked smug. "I took down his license plate number. Then I had someone at the DMV run the number. You're not the only one with contacts, you know."

"Good investigative work." He gave her the compliment before leaning in closer and pointing his finger in his face. "Forget everything you know about Ed Mercer, okay?"

"Okay, but maybe I should go along with you." Her eyes lit up. "I could be your back up."

"Ab-so-freaking-lutely not." He ran his hand through his hair and glanced at the clock. He for damn sure didn't have time for this. "Look, I'll call you tomorrow and explain."

"Don't bother." She turned back to the sink.

Irritation itched at him. Damned reverse psychology. "Annabel... don't make this any more difficult than it already is."

"I'm not," she declared. "I'm making it easy. Don't come over. Don't call. We did what we did. Now you have to go to work. The end."

"I don't want you to have regrets." He couldn't live with himself if she regretted what had happened between them. He was almost certain he could talk her into seeing him again if he just had a little more time.

"I don't." Her voice bit off the words so tightly that he didn't believe her for one second.

She might get physically hurt if she went with him, but leaving her emotionally bruised felt all wrong, too. But he had no choice, damn it! He'd make one last stab at setting things right between them and then he'd get out of there. Tugging on her shoulders, he turned her to face him. She did, but she took her own sweet time shaking excess water from her hands and drying them on a dishtowel.

"Walk me to the door."

Great, now she looked vulnerable and dejected. He didn't want her to feel either one of those things because of him. He curled his fingers around hers, encouraged that she let them remain.

Hell, it was part of his job to think on his feet, to come up with the right words for any situation. Normally, this would be the time for something light, something glib. Something meaningless like "Had a good time. I'll call you." But the one time he would have meant it, she'd taken the punch out of that line.

"Thanks for tonight," he said once they reached the door. "It was special."

"For me, too." She crossed her arms and shivered.

He wanted more than anything to stay and warm her up again from the inside out. "I wouldn't leave like this if I didn't have to."

"Yes, you would. That's your pattern. I was expecting it."

Wow, that put him in his place. "Look," he said, more frustrated than he'd been in a long while. "I can't take you with me. It'll probably be one long bore. But just in case it's not, it doesn't involve you and I don't want you getting hurt." He lifted her chin and looked into clear blue eyes that beckoned him into uncharted depths. "I'll call you tomorrow?"

Unflinching, she answered, "I really don't want you to."

He didn't allow the finality of her words to register. He was a firm believer in tomorrow. "Then I'll see you next week at *Let's Talk.*"

"Oh, right, the follow-up show. I'll see you then—if I don't run into you first."

He could see the effort that went into her small joke and he chuckled, dropping a last kiss on her lips. "In the best interest of my Porsche, I hope you don't." He opened the door and stepped outside. "Bye, Annabel."

"Be careful," she said, kissing him lightly.

"I will." He paused, ready to take off.

"Here, take this." Holding the door open, she thrust a small packet in his hand. "You'll need it before I will."

By the time he realized it was the last remaining condom, he was alone on the porch. A solid oak barrier standing between them.

"Annabel!" He rapped his fist against the door. The porch light went dark. The foyer light immediately followed.

With a shake of his head, he turned and ran through the slicing rain to the waiting limo.

Annabel's body thrummed with frustration as she closed the door on Max and ignored the sound of his voice calling her name.

He'd promised her all night, damn it!

She hadn't wanted him to leave on an adventure without her, with the promises unfulfilled, and one condom left unused. Just like a man to stick her with kitchen duty while he went off on another adventure.

Her every compulsive instinct yelled at her to tidy up. For once, some small part of her rebelled against the notion. She didn't want to be the good little girl left behind to do the grunt work anymore.

With her chin raised, she headed up the stairs, but jumped at a chirping sound on the bottom step. She looked down to discover Max's cell phone. She scooped it up. Hmmm. The caller might be another woman looking for late-night company.

Or it could be important.

An emergency even.

Or an update on the stakeout.

"Hello?"

"Who's this?" demanded a voice as rough as sandpaper. "Where's Max?"

"Who's this?"

"Tell Max—No! Don't tell Max anything. Crap, I shoulda never got involved in this mess." Click.

Well! She didn't know what to make of the message, but Max would. It might have been Mercer. It might mean trouble. She looked out just in time to see the limo's taillights round the corner.

If she hurried, maybe she could still catch him.

She slipped into the kick-ass gorgeous shoes she'd worn to the ceremony, pulled her raincoat out of the closet, grabbed her car keys, and rushed toward the garage.

Max imagined even James Bond didn't arrive at many stakeouts in a chauffeur-driven limousine, but what the hell?

A motley assortment of teenaged boys on the corner—maybe gang-bangers, probably up to no-good—scattered like cockroaches when Eduardo dropped off Max a couple of blocks from the alleged crime in progress. Max pulled the lapels of his tux over his white shirt and kept to the deep, dark shadows while he edged toward the city warehouse. The pouring rain added another layer of fun to the adventure. Soaked to the skin, he ducked into a protected doorway with an unobstructed view.

As Mercer had predicted, a nondescript moving van backed up to the loading dock. Ghouls in dark clothing hunched their shoulders against the downpour, scurrying in and out of the building, filling the truck with large, unwieldy boxes.

Keeping an eye out for Mercer, Max about jumped out of his skin when a mountain-sized human tapped him on the shoulder.

"Damn, Roger! Don't sneak up on me like that!"

The mountain chuckled with a deep rumble. "Whatever you say, man. I thought we were recording this on the sly. But next time, I'll just pull into the parking lot and honk the horn."

"Point taken," Max grumbled. "Do you have a long-angle night lens? We need to be able to read the labels on those boxes and capture as many faces as possible."

"I've got the distance for that, but the rain's a problem. And the lack of light." Roger held his plastic-covered video camera to his eye and recorded for a minute before shaking his head. "I can make out the words on the boxes, but the faces are fuzzy. I need to get closer. Maybe I can get on that roof next door without attracting attention."

Warily, Max looked from the roof to the cameraman and back. "Uh huh, did you bring an extension ladder?"

"I thought you could give me a boost."

"Me and what forklift?"

"Listen, do you want my help or not? It's the middle of the night, it's raining, and believe it or not, you weren't the only one gettin' lucky. So if you don't need me, I've got better things to do."

"I want your help." Keeping an eye on the activity at the warehouse, Max scowled. "How do you know what I was doing?"

"I saw who you left the ceremony with. And seeing as how my invitation for tonight's caper didn't indicate black tie, I don't imagine you came here from your own lonely bed." Roger pulled a black T-shirt out of his backpack and tossed it to Max. "Here, put this on over that neon sign of a shirt."

"Uh, about who I was with..." He dodged behind the cameraman, took off his jacket, and tugged the black T-shirt into place. "She wouldn't want—I wouldn't want her to think—"

Roger clapped a hand on Max's shoulder and turned him toward the corner as he slipped back into his jacket. "It's cool, dude. I won't say anything."

They fell silent as they closed in on the action. Closer than Max wanted to be. Still watching for Mercer, he occasionally thought he heard a footstep behind him. But when he turned to look, there was no one. Before long, his dress shoes began to squish, and the foot without the sock developed blisters.

The two men angled around behind a building cattycorner to the warehouse. A couple of orange road barrels lay on their sides. Max's sense of unease grew. They should have stayed where they'd been in the first place.

Hell, he should have stayed where he'd been when he got

the call. Even in this stinking back alley that smelled like mildew, piss, and dead rats, Annabel's sweet fresh scent drifted around him. It was all he could do not to abandon the lure of breaking this story wide open and turning around instead. He wanted to go back to her and pick up where they'd left off, but this was his job. And something rotten was definitely going down.

"Let's roll one of those barrels down to that fire escape," Roger stage-whispered.

Stuck for a better idea, Max agreed. Roger attached a strap to his camera and slung it over his neck to free his hands, but the burden hampered his movements. Every sound magnified in Max's mind as they grappled with the weighted barrel, scraped it across gravel, and ended up rolling it across the cameraman's toe.

"Holy bat shit." He released the words in a hiss while hopping up and down with his foot in his hand.

A slim shadow separated itself from a sheltered doorway, and Max instinctively crouched into attack position. Flinging himself forward, recognition would have halted him, but momentum sent him crashing full speed into Annabel. For a second he thought his previous longing for her had conjured her image, but his arms around her sweet shoulders verified her presence.

"What the hell are you doing here?" Stunned, he pulled her into a hug despite his displeasure.

"Getting wet." She snuggled into the embrace.

"*Why* are you here?"

"You left this at my house." She pulled his cell phone out of her trench coat pocket. "Some guy called right after you left. I thought it might be Mercer."

"What did he say?"

"It was disjointed, but I thought you should know he was trying to reach you."

Annabel's presence made the whole scene even more surreal. He tried to follow her words, but he felt off balance and out of sync. "How did you know where I was going?"

"I followed you."

"What is this? A frigging parade?" He threw up his hands, uncertain whether to shake her or kiss her. A premonition of doom washed over him. Whatever happened next, he had to get rid of her before this escapade turned into a major shit-show. He took the phone out of her hand and dropped it into a pocket. "Thanks. Now, go away." The words came out sternly, but he ruined the effect with a swift kiss that somehow deepened and lengthened and expanded into a distraction that grabbed his full attention until Roger tapped him on the shoulder.

When he finally managed to pull away from her, the cameraman gave him a big thumb's up.

"But I can help." She moved to one side of the barrel. "Let's just get this into place, then I'll leave. Where do you want it?"

Roger accepted her presence and assistance as a matter of course. Her added muscle helped not a bit, but the three of them wrestled it into place. Max's niggling worry for her safety mounted.

"Now go," he told her.

"Sure. I'll just be the lookout until Roger gets up on the roof. I assume you want to avoid those guys loading that truck at the warehouse."

"No," he began. "I want you to—" He stopped talking because she'd already snuck around the corner and out of sight. Damn.

Max didn't know exactly when he'd lost control of the evening, but it was probably when he'd arrived at Annabel's more than seven hours before and caught sight of her dressed like Snow White's naughty sister.

He turned to watch the cameraman's first attempt at hoisting himself on top of the barrel. A whoosh of air escaped him after his failed leap.

"They're taller than they look when you're driving beside them on the highway." Roger rubbed the potbelly that was his biggest obstacle. "You're going to have to boost me up."

Max linked his hands into a stirrup and lifted when Roger put his sneakered foot inside. Roger's landing on top of the barrel didn't get them home free. Struggling to stand, he looked a bit like a circus elephant balancing on a performance pedestal. Even on tiptoe, he could barely reach the fire escape.

Just as Max decided to give up and call him back to the ground, the cameraman managed a one-handed grasp of the bottom rung and shinnied up to the next level.

"I got it, buddy." He hoisted the camera onto his shoulder. "Man, oh, man, you're not gonna believe what we've got here.

This is better than your wildest dreams."

Max's hair stood up on the back of his neck. "What? Who can you see? What are they taking?"

"We're takin' everything but the Mayor's new computer, and we might take that too," came a gruff voice from behind him. "Too bad you and Fatso won't be around to tell about it."

# Chapter Eleven

"Fatso?" Roger's voice floated down from the rooftop like an offended archangel.

Max jerked his head to the left. A long-bladed knife sliced through the sensitive skin beneath his ear. Ignoring the sharp sting, he shoved an elbow backward into the mushy gut of a black-clad villain and hotfooted it down the alley. Out of the corner of his eye, he spotted another criminal slithering up the fire escape with the ease of a lizard.

"Take off, Rog!" He hoped the cameraman had an escape route he could handle across the damp roofs, but concern for Annabel crowded out every other thought. Max heard the thud of footsteps behind him as his own assailant rebounded from his tumble and rounded the corner.

She wasn't visible in the alcove she'd melted into earlier. He hoped she had the sense to stay out of sight. If not, his best bet was to lead the scoundrel as far away from her as possible.

Max had combed the area carefully in the past week, preparing for just such an unlikely event as this. If he picked up some speed and made it around the next corner before his tail caught up with him, he could disappear into an old storm sewer while Swifty passed him by, then get a jump on him from behind. Maybe... Probably... Hopefully.

Swifty's breath turned into a labored huff and puff. His pursuit flagged. The corner loomed ahead of Max. He made the turn and ran flat into Annabel... An Annabel holding a three-foot-long two-by-four over her head like an avenging angel.

Without slowing, he took her hand and pulled her along with him, desperately trying to come up with a Plan B. A brick wall up ahead sported an opening with a rusty, but unlocked metal gate. Pushing through it, he left the gate ajar and sent Annabel to one side while he positioned himself on the other. He motioned for her to crouch down. Pulling her stocking from his pocket, he gave her one end and gestured for her to hold it to the ground.

Seconds later, Swifty came lumbering through, wheezing like an asthmatic fish. Max and Annabel raised the stocking six inches from the ground, tripped the thief, and sent him lurching into a face full of mud and gravel. Max leapt forward and stomped on the hand with the knife, kicking the blade free.

The creep made a grab for Max's ankle, but Annabel whacked him on the back of the head with the two-by-four, knocking him right out. Tossing the board aside, she dropped down and rammed her knees into the middle of the jerk's back, forcing the breath from his lungs. She straddled him like a bareback rider, providing Max with an eyeful of thigh.

Terrified by the thought of Annabel so close to harm's way, Max dropped down next to her and yanked the twitching and groaning thug's hands behind his back. "Hold still, slime ball," he ordered. "Get off him, Annabel."

"What?"

"You heard me." Roughly, he bound Swifty's wrists with the stocking. "Get off him," he repeated as she remained in place.

Gripped by adrenalin and anger at Annabel for intentionally throwing herself into danger surged up inside him, his hands began to shake. He could only risk sidelong glances in her direction for fear he'd lose it completely and throttle her instead of the prone miscreant.

"Give me the belt off your raincoat," he demanded through clenched teeth.

She looked soaked, bedraggled, beautiful, and delicious, and he was sporting wood again. All he wanted to do was drag her off somewhere and wrap himself around her. But now was *not* the time. Jeez, he was farther gone over her than he thought.

"I need your belt to bind his feet." He gestured for her to hurry.

She moved to do so, but stopped with her hands hovering over the buckle. Sirens wailed in the distance, drawing closer by the second, and he heaved a sigh of relief. Roger must have managed to call for help.

"The thing is..." She drew his attention to her long, bare legs as she shifted position. Unfastening the belt, the coat dropped open, and he knew what *the thing* was.

Even in the dark alley, under an overcast and dark sky, with very little ambient light, his mouth watered over the gleam of creamy skin. Her shiny purple panties and tank top darkened and glued to her skin as the rain cascaded down.

"You came out to get yourself into you didn't know what kind of trouble dressed like every adolescent's wet dream?" He quickly secured Swifty's feet and helped Annabel stand.

"Adolescents dream about trench coats?" She lifted her chin defiantly, but he could have sworn if the light were better that he would have seen her blush.

"Covering nothing but your smokin' hot body and sexy silk underwear? You betcha." He didn't want to hang onto his anger and terror, but worried that if he let go of it, his sense of relief would catapult him into hysterical laughter. Or unwise declarations. "Why didn't you get dressed first?"

"There wasn't time! When your caller hung up, I grabbed my coat, shoes, and keys to take off after you."

That was either the bravest or the stupidest thing he'd ever known anyone to do. And she'd done it for him. Amazing.

He hugged her tight and kissed her, too, soaking up the relief of having her safe. And having her near. "I think I liked you better when you were afraid of your own shadow."

"No, you didn't." Her voice muffled against his shoulder.

No, he hadn't. He shook his head, unable to realign the image of the boring, predictable Annabel he'd known for the last three years with this new-and-improved, more tantalizing, determined version she'd morphed into in the last two weeks.

"No, but it was better for my heart." A whole lot better. And safer. This daring balls-to-the-wall Annabel posed a definite threat to life as he knew it. He took her by the shoulders and stepped back, torn between shaking her and holding onto her forever. "In the future, you'll have to land somewhere in the middle of timid and intrepid, okay? You scared me half to death."

"Imagine how I feel." Her fingers grazed the skin below his ear. "You're the one bleeding."

"It's just a scratch." He hoped. "Don't worry about it."

As a cop car pulled into the alley with lights flashing, duty called. He released her and drew the edges of her coat together.

"Button that thing up. Do you want to stay and run the risk of being mistaken for a hooker, or do you want to slip away now?"

Annabel let herself into her house slightly before dawn. Thank heavens she hadn't been arrested for prostitution. It was a close thing until Max's biker friend, Detective Dan Kirby, arrived on the scene.

He'd begun to question her about the night's events, but after a few whispered words from Max, the detective let her go. When last she saw Max, he and Roger were recording a piece in front of the warehouse. Good to know Roger had managed to escape unharmed. Apparently, she'd walked into an ongoing investigation that would headline tomorrow's news and result in some high-ranking political arrests.

Her pride in the role she played diminished now that she entered her empty house. She found everything there as she had left it. Silently mocking her, as if nothing special had happened.

And everything had happened.

Sex, crime, adventure. Love... maybe. Maybe not.

On autopilot, she drifted into the kitchen. But somewhere along the way her obsession with tidiness deserted her. With a sweeping glance at the mess she'd let Max make—helped him make, really—her heart flipped over.

Every dribble, every crumb, every splatter became proof of the incredible hours they'd spent together. Unwilling to erase the tiniest bit of tangible evidence, she turned off the light and trudged upstairs.

The scene in her bedroom depressed her more than the kitchen. The smell of sex clung to the room like a musky perfume. Damp and discouraged, she threw herself across the rumpled sheets and inhaled deeply.

Max had wallowed over every square inch of this bed, and she breathed deeply of the masculine scent. Closing her eyes, she absorbed his essence through every pore.

She'd take a shower then sleep in the guest room, after she soaked up a little bit more of him. In just a minute. Spreading her arms wide, she savored her body's unfamiliar hum of bone-deep sexual satisfaction and adrenaline aftermath.

Mad Max Williams, a man of practically legendary lovemaking skills, had taken her to a level of sensuality she'd never experienced. His influence had spurred her to a new appreciation of sex and adventure. She should thank him for both. Were there Mylar balloons designed for such an occasion?

In lieu of a card or balloons, letting him go without demanding a commitment from him was the least she could do to show her gratitude. Max probably hated clingy, overly grateful women unable to keep a couple of explosive orgasms in the proper perspective as much as he hated celibacy.

The evening had been fun for both of them. Nothing more than sex as usual for Max.

She needed to remember that.

She could never let herself think the evening meant more than it had. Letting herself consider being in love with him caused her major palpitations.

Because he was leaving.

Soon.

And thinking she was in love with him would transform her from merely boring and lonely to downright pathetic. Easy prey for the first man who'd shown her any attention in three years. The first man who'd looked at her and seen something beneath the uptight persona and baggy clothes, something inside her that wanted to be so much more than a former wife, an almost mother, and a part-time documentarian.

She wanted no more half measures in her life.

If Max had been astute enough to see beneath the disguise, to see the woman she wanted to be, then someone else—someone who wanted to stick around—would be able to see that, too. Now that she knew the truth about herself, she could be the person Max had seen. Freer, softer, more flexible.

More *fun*, to use one of Max's favorite words.

But that someone wouldn't be Max, and Max was the one she loved.

Well, damn.

She tossed a pillow across the room. She hadn't meant to admit that. Even to herself.

Seeing him leave would hurt, but she was glad she hadn't let him wander in and out of her life as another lost opportunity. The time she'd spent with him thrilled her all the way down to her toes. *So, why the tears?*

Covering her face with her hands, she cried wet, selfish tears, harder than she'd cried since she was eighteen and found out she couldn't go to film school in New York. She wanted to rail against life and injustice, unfair responsibilities and lost chances, but decided it would take too much effort.

She banished the drama, wiped her eyes on a sheet corner and recognized a vague, disconnected feeling. *What next?* Sleep seemed out of the question. Might as well drown her misery and plan her future in a long tub soak.

Before she summoned the energy to get up, a cold splash dampened her toes. And then a drip-drop of water soon turned into a trickle. She jerked her feet aside, peering upward.

Damn. A leaking roof.

Right over her bed.

"Great."

She went in search of a bucket, giving serious thought to the idea of selling the house. It was paid for, sure, but the upkeep comprised a pretty hefty amount each year. Carl had bought the house the year Carly was born, and Annabel didn't know what the girl would think about giving up the only home she'd ever known. While Carl's life insurance would pay for her four years at The Ohio State University, the sale of the house would go a long way toward covering her medical school fees. That was probably another ticklish conversation they needed to have soon.

Annabel sighed. No point in adding one more thing to tonight's worry list.

She'd lost an award, a lover, and part of her roof all in one evening. If this kind of luck held true, next, she'd lose her job.

After a long soak with a glass of wine and a boring book, Annabel stumbled to the kitchen in a dispirited fog. Too tired to attend yoga class, she lingered over multiple cups of tea instead. Watching the local news on her laptop, she kept her eyes riveted on the screen when Carly poked her head in the back door around ten o'clock.

"All alone?" the chipper teen asked.

Annabel merely nodded. The disastrous condition of the kitchen caught Carly's attention.

"Holy guacamole, what happened in here?"

To prevent Carly from detecting any hint of the previous night's sex-capades on Annabel's face, she kept her focus on the news. "I fixed a midnight breakfast and was too tired to clean up afterward."

"Honestly?" Carly peered around wide-eyed. "Are you sick? You never let *me* leave a mess like this."

"And you can see why." Annabel frowned at the mess around her. "In retrospect, it was a mistake."

Carly moved the strawberry jam from the place Max had occupied the night before and sat down. "Thanks for texting me about the awards. We saw some Community First footage on the late news last night. You and Max looked awesome together." She reached out and pushed the laptop's screen down. "I'm sorry you didn't win."

"Thanks, I got your text, too. That was sweet."

"Are you okay, Anna?"

She worked her throat a couple of times, but finally her answer emerged with a stiff smile. "I'm fine."

"And how was Max?"

*Fabulous*, Annabel wanted to say, but she supposed Carly's question didn't refer to his post-ceremony performance. "He seemed okay."

"Did he have breakfast with you?"

With two used plates and cups on the table there was no way to deny it. "Yeah, we both needed company and a little cheering up."

Carly sat forward, eager for details. "How long did he stay?"

"Awhile."

"Annabel!" she huffed. "You forget that I'm almost eighteen. If you want to stop treating me like a twelve-year-old who's never been kissed, you can."

Annabel rested her head in her hand, choosing her answer with care. "It's not so much your age, sweetie, as our relationship. I'm used to being the parent, and I still think I need to protect you."

"My mom told me about the birds and bees a long time ago, you know."

"Hey! *I* told you about the birds and the bees."

Carly smirked. "Yeah, but her version was a lot better than yours."

"Oh, really?" Annabel's eyebrows skyrocketed.

"You've only been married to Dad, and so she knows more."

"She's only been married to your dad, too."

"Yeah, but that was a long time ago, and no offense, but

she's made up for it since."

"And she's shared details of her sex life with you?" Annabel was past being appalled at Belinda's idea of sound parenting, but she wished she'd known about this sooner. No telling what inappropriate stories Carly had heard.

"Some, so it's all right if you want to talk to me, too. You're always going on about how knowledge is power."

"I wasn't talking about sex!"

"Yeah, but I always thought that was because you didn't know much about it. Mom says even though you have a college education, you may not be an expert on this subject."

Annabel found herself caught between laughter and outrage. Maybe they were right about her sexual expertise, but she'd learned a lot in the last twenty-four hours. And she wasn't about to share that information with Carly.

"How long did Max stay? Did you sleep with him? Did he spend the night?" Luckily the barrage of questions came too closely together to be answered individually.

"Until about two thirty. No! And no!" Annabel blurted out responses just to stop the flow. True enough, they'd planned for him to spend the night, but he hadn't. And there had been absolutely no sleeping.

"Did *anything* happen?"

"Nothing worth talking about." Her cheeks reddened, and she knew from Carly's grin that the girl noticed.

"Then why are you blushing?"

"We really can't discuss this. I still think of you as a teenage soccer-jock, not a young Dr. Phil."

Carly leaned forward, a young beautiful girl, but nearly a woman. "I've had more boyfriends in the last three years than you have."

Annabel remembered those boyfriends and remembered all the late nights watching the clock until the teenager got home. Still… "Max was wonderful, a gentleman, and he got called away for work before we got around to cleaning up this mess."

"Oh, Annabel." Carly shook her head in disappointment. "Only you would go out with a hunk like Max and send him home alone."

Annabel fidgeted with the zipper pull on her robe, eager to halt the discussion. "Carly, I really don't want to talk about this."

Her stepdaughter studied her for a full ten seconds. "Why

are you so upset if nothing happened? Is it because you expected something to happen and it didn't? Or did he make a pass and you didn't know how to handle it?"

"Of course not! Are these more of your mother's ideas?"

"No, I'm just saying... You were used to Dad."

Annabel straightened in her chair. "What do you mean by that?"

"Well, he was a professor of *literature*." She wrinkled her nose. "Smart and sweet, but not real involved, and since there were very few PDAs, I'm guessing, not very demonstrative. And no offense, but Mom once told me that he was about as exciting in bed as a dead poodle."

"A dead poodle? What does that mean?"

"I don't know." Carly got up and opened the fridge, scrounging around for a container of yogurt. "I thought it was one of those expressions adults use that don't make sense unless you understand the context. Maybe she said *wet* poodle. He was about as exciting as a wet poodle."

"Did she say "wet noodle?"" The description didn't flatter Carl, but at least it didn't border on necrophilia. Or bestiality.

"Wet noodle! Yes, that's it." At that, Carly must have caught a glimpse of Annabel's disapproval. "Eewww. Believe me, that's a lot more than a girl wants to know about her father. Please, don't feel the need to confirm, deny, or share similar confidences."

Annabel had no intention of doing so. Her thoughts reeled wildly away from the direction the conversation had taken.

"You know I love you, Anna. I can't imagine my life without you, but..." Carly bit her lip and dropped her gaze before finishing in a rush. "One thing I always wondered is why you married him. He was crazy about you, in his own quiet way, but I don't know what you saw in him."

Many people had been surprised about the mismatch in their ages, but it hadn't seemed odd to her. "He gave me so much, honey. A home, security, love, all the things I lacked after my parents died."

"But did you love him?"

"In some ways, I did." Annabel smiled at the thought of her husband's many fine qualities. "I admired his intelligence, his gentleness, his dependability. He really needed me in his life, and I liked that." She'd found the idea fulfilling at the time, but she'd given up a lot of herself to please Carl and make the marriage work. And she hadn't realized until last night how much had been missing. "And if I hadn't married him, I wouldn't have you in my life."

"I'm glad you were happy with him, and for purely selfish reasons, I'm glad you married him."

Annabel pulled her into a hug, pushing away pointless regrets at the same time. "Me, too, honey."

"But Max, now." Carly awarded Annabel with an impish grin. "He looks like a complete stud. He's got a sexy smile and a great butt. And I love how he follows you with his eyes. I thought from the way he looked last night when he saw you in that dress that he wouldn't be able to keep his hands off of you." She waited expectantly, but Annabel's tongue remained glued to the roof of her mouth.

Carly shrugged. "Of course, if you say nothing happened, I believe you, because you never lie. But I hoped you'd have someone special in your life."

"I have you in my life, and you're special."

"That's not the kind of 'special' I mean. I'll be leaving soon, and I wanted you to have someone you could count on besides me."

"Well, I appreciate the thought, sweetie. Really I do, but I don't need a man in my life to be happy, and Max would only be a temporary fix at best."

"Yeah," Carly said, laughing. "But he'd be good for some excitement."

"Until he's gone."

"Gone? Where's he going?"

Annabel lifted her cup for a sip of stone cold tea. She returned it to the saucer with a clink. "News people tend to move from market to market. It's not a very stable lifestyle."

"Oh, shoot," Carly huffed. "I hadn't thought of that. Where would he go after here?"

"New York, maybe."

"New York! That's great! You should go, too. There are plenty of career opportunities in New York."

"Sure. Documentary companies there are dying to give high-budget projects to unknown women with nothing more to recommend them than having been an also-ran for a local media award."

"You have more to recommend you than that." Carly shook her head. "The only thing keeping you from trying is you."

"That and the desire to keep a roof over my head." Although her current roof required about twenty grand she didn't have to get it reshingled before the next deluge.

"All right, maybe that plan's too aggressive for you. Max and New York are big leaps for someone with your timid nature, but I'll keep thinking. Maybe I can scout up someone more suitable for you. The new boys' soccer coach is built like a Greek statue, thirty, and single."

*Timid nature?* Ouch, that hurt. Especially after her recent progress. Of course, Carly hadn't seen Annabel in her trench coat last night, eluding a criminal and aiding in his capture. And she wasn't at liberty to mention anything about it yet.

"Or," Annabel said, deflecting the suggestion, "I can decide what to do with my life all by myself."

"Yeah, right." Carly shook her head and snorted, as if she found the possibility farfetched. She stood and stretched. "I'm going to take a shower, then head over to school for soccer practice."

"How long will you be gone?"

"Back by two. How about you?"

"I'm feeling lazy today." Annabel yawned to emphasize the point. "Maybe I'll just stay around here."

"Says the lady who thinks she can manage her own love life." Carly left the kitchen with a parting shot. "You won't find any available males if you don't get out there and look."

Annabel knew that. She did. She just couldn't handle it today. Dropping her head in her hands, she rubbed her temples and contemplated cleaning the kitchen.

Out in the foyer, Carly's footsteps paused halfway up the stairs, then stomped back to the kitchen.

"Uh huh," she said, with one fist planted on her hip and a bow tie dangling from the fingertips of her other hand. "What is *this*?"

Annabel willed herself to stay calm. "Max's tie. He hates wearing them and says he feels like they're strangling him, so he took it off when we got here. I guess he forgot it."

"That makes sense." Carly lifted her other hand from her hip and revealed a black dress sock balled up in her palm. "Does he feel strangled wearing socks, too?"

*Oh, God, busted!* Teenagers were far too knowing these days to let a parent get away with anything. Annabel expected Carly to ground her any minute now.

"I guess so." She plucked both items from Carly's grasp. "I'll make sure he gets them back."

To Annabel's vast disappointment, her phone remained silent throughout most of Sunday. And when it did ring, it wasn't who she wanted to hear from. No calls, no texts from Max. Her phone worked both ways though. She debated calling him. A daring step for her, but she didn't want him to interpret the action as needy, or desperate, or smitten.

No matter how much she wanted him, they were still all wrong for one another. She could never be with someone who treated women as callously as he'd treated DeeDee, but then again… Now that she knew him better, she couldn't picture him actually treating a woman that way. Rumors could be wrong. And DeeDee never actually said she was hung up on Max. Or that the baby was his. Maybe Annabel had mistakenly assumed those things.

She stewed over it for a few minutes before pulling up DeeDee's Facebook page to catch up on her recent posts. Loved her new job. Cute baby. Newly engaged. To her baby's father, Jonathan Andrews.

Ah ha! Jonathan used to work on the WKLK news team with Max. The guy had been married when he lived and worked in Cincinnati. That provided an explanation for Max not wanting to explain more about his relationship with DeeDee. Maybe he hadn't really had one, just provided a smokescreen for the relationship between DeeDee and Jonathan. Or he loaned her a sympathetic ear when she needed one. Now, that made more sense.

If the grapevine had been wrong about Max and DeeDee, it probably misfired about Max and the intern, too. Annabel would check it out later, but she felt more confident that it had been completely misconstrued.

With the first objection swept away, she still wasn't sure he was interested in her, or that they had any kind of future.

After another fretful night, she put the sock and tie in her messenger bag and took them to work with her on Monday. She stuffed them in her desk drawer before anyone could see her mooning over them like an idiot. Occasionally, she reached in and rubbed the tie between her fingers like a lucky rabbit's foot.

A couple of times—or a couple of *dozen* times—she started to call Max, but each time she returned the phone to her pocket undialed.

If she called him, he'd think she couldn't resist him. He'd think she'd use any trumped up excuse to contact him. He'd think she couldn't stop thinking about him.

And of course, she couldn't, whether she wanted to or not. His face loomed everywhere today. Not just on television, but in the newspaper too. This morning's *Enquirer* blared its praise of his exposure of corruption in the city government. Key figures had been brought in for questioning. Arrests had been made.

Still, she couldn't forget she'd let him see her at her most vulnerable. Let him see her with her guard down.

Let him see her naked.

Even editing her latest project in her tiny but tidy office, her mind filled with images of Max in every pose from unaware to interested to aroused. And it was pointless to let her thoughts linger on any of those areas.

His latest coup would probably cement the network deal. He'd be moving to New York any minute now.

The Big Apple.

Good for him.

She'd dreamed of living and working in New York once upon a time. Carly's recent prodding reminded Annabel of that forgotten goal and many other dreams she'd put on hold. A temporary hold that had lengthened from one or two years to a full dozen.

Just because there wouldn't be anything to tie her to Cincinnati after Carly left didn't mean Annabel should give up the security of her low-paying, unfulfilling, dead-end job and sell her paid-for-but-in-need-of-a new roof home to take a long shot at achieving some vague and unpredictable dreams. Disheartened, she sighed and rubbed Max's tie again.

Maybe Carly was right. Maybe Annabel lacked the guts.

An intern named Brittany, not much older than Carly, came in to drop off a stack of mail. Annabel usually took the time to encourage the girl's interest in producing documentaries. The girl was nice, talented, too, but prone to gossip.

"Too bad about the award," Brittany said. "It would've been awesome to win. I was rooting for you."

"Thanks." Annabel didn't look up, uneager to chat today. "Maybe next time."

"I saw you on the news." The intern headed for the door. "Fabulous dress."

"Thanks, I liked it too." *And so had Max.* Annabel flipped through the mail, but stopped short. "Brittany, wait."

The intern stopped with her hand on the door. "Something I can do to help?"

"Just something I was wondering about."

"Okay." Brittany came back and leaned her hip against Annabel's desk.

"You go to UC, right?" She set the stack of mail aside. "Do you know a girl who was a news intern last year named, uh, I think it was, Miranda?"

"The one that was fired? Sure, I knew her. She left school though."

Annabel hated to ask. She cautioned herself not to, but… "Do you know why?"

"Why she was dismissed? Or why she left school? Same reason, either way." The intern dropped her voice to a whisper. "She was into some heavy drugs. I heard one of the reporters caught her doing something stupid at work. Snorting heroin is the unconfirmed story. They say he tried to get her into rehab, but when he caught her with the same shit a second time, she was history."

"I'm sorry to hear it." Annabel knew too many kids fell prey to drugs for too many reasons. Not just at-risk kids from the *Challenging Destiny* high school, but girls from Carly's high school, from their neighborhood, and even their church. "She had a promising future."

"I guess." Brittany chewed her thumbnail a minute. "Uh, Annabel, I hope she gets her life straightened out, but until she gets help she could really spell trouble. Are you thinking of hiring her to help you out here? In addition to me? Or in place of me?"

"No, nothing like that. You're doing a great job, but someone mentioned her to me the other day. I just wondered what happened. If there was something I could do to help her."

"No offense, but if she wouldn't listen to Max, I doubt if she'd listen to you either."

Annabel went very still except for the chills running down her spine. "Max Williams was the reporter who tried to get her into rehab?"

"Yeah, he's kind of like a mentor for the interns there. He always does stuff like that to help people. Didn't you know?" Brittany looked surprised.

"I didn't know." *But I should have.*

"I saw you went to the ceremony with him the other night. That was really cool. Doesn't that mean you two are friends?"

"We are, but he keeps surprising me."

"I'll bet." Brittany smirked, but then straightened. "Oops, I've got a class in half an hour. I need to deliver the rest of this mail then get over to campus. See ya."

Annabel leaned back in her chair and chewed her lip, distressed at how she'd misjudged Max all the way around. While she thought of ways to make amends, she reached for the stack of mail, adjusted it neatly, tapped the edges, sorted it by size, and then placed it squarely in the center of her desk. Obsessive straightening, an old habit of hers.

One large canary yellow envelope stood out among the supply catalogs and industry mags. She flipped it over. The return address made her heart skip a beat. She ripped the envelope open and scanned the contents.

Dear Ms. Morgan, We have recently reviewed your...

*Oh, my!* She pressed a hand against her flipping stomach and gulped several deep breaths before continuing. Her gaze scanned the incredible news quickly.

Extraordinary talent... Limited class size... Willing to offer you...

*Oh, mygosh! Oh, mygosh! Oh, mygosh!* She clutched the letter against her chest and danced a quick two-step around the cramped office.

Over a year ago she'd sent audition footage and a resume to her hero, legendary cinematographer Lance Foreman. She'd never expected anything beyond a form rejection, but now she held in her shaking hands an invitation to attend Lance's eight-week course at UCLA.

*Yes!* She pumped her fist in the air and rocketed back and forth from one side of her small space to the other. Think of how much she could learn from him! The opportunity beamed brightly as the highlight of her fledgling career.

And if she took the course, a little voice inside her head teased, she'd be in a much stronger position to go to New York, or anywhere else she wanted. Maybe with a recommendation from Lance Foreman himself.

With her hand on her cell phone, intent on calling Max to share her good news, her desk phone rang. She jumped about a foot in the air.

"You busy?" her boss asked over the pounding in her ears.

Proving he didn't have a surveillance camera in her office, as she'd often suspected. If he did, he'd know just how unproductive her day had been. Unless he considered obsessing over Max a good use of her time. Or gossiping with interns. Or celebrating offers from outside sources. She clicked on the screen that had gone to black. "Just editing this piece on local church steeples for the Historical Society."

"How's that going?"

She bit her lip and refused to tell an out-right lie. "Slowly."

He grunted. "Drop that and come down to my office."

"Yes, sir!" Being at Howard Lasting's beck and call was just another one of the super perks that came with earning a paycheck. She felt a moment's unease, wondering if her premonition about getting fired was about to come true.

She moved through the no-frills production area to the less familiar luxury of the business offices where Howard held the monetary reins on the staff's creative urges. His secretary nodded and waved Annabel into his private domain.

"What's up?" She dropped into the stiff-backed visitor's chair opposite Howard's ergonomic marvel.

"Too bad about the award." He reached behind his desk and retrieved two bottles of Evian from the mini-bar.

He held one in her direction, but she refused with a shake of her head. Whatever he wanted to say, she didn't want to prolong the suspense. "I thought I had a shot."

"You did good work," he acknowledged.

"Thanks." The unexpected praise surprised her and put her on guard for the upcoming discussion.

He leaned back in his chair and flapped his tie. He always liked to pause for dramatic effect. Annabel leaned back and straightened her cuffs. Point, counterpoint.

"I've been thinking about your place in the organization," he said at last.

"Ah." Expecting the worst, Annabel gripped the arms of her chair. Both dreading the news and welcoming it. If she lost her job, she'd be free to attend Foreman's class. She'd might have no other choice than to relocate. She could move to Chicago or Los Angeles.

Or New York.

Her pulse almost tripped over itself as she considered the possibilities.

"I've decided to let you produce that motorcycle documentary you pitched me the other day," he said.

That jerked her back into the moment. "What?"

"You've paid your dues here. It's time to see what else you can do."

"Thank you." She would have jumped through hoops for the opportunity a few days earlier, but now she felt a monumental lack of enthusiasm.

Her mind actually wandered as he went over the details. Instead of basking in her triumph or employing some harmless flattery to get him to increase her budget, she thanked him for the opportunity. She made an excuse to leave his office, offered a casual, "Let me think about it," and breezed out the door.

She should have sang and danced her way down the halls as she returned to her office, but her feet dragged in a dirge-like shuffle.

At her desk, she retrieved a Project Initiation Form from a file drawer and paused before filling it out. Normally, the formality of completing the form would have thrilled her to her toes, but not today.

Now she had a really good excuse to call Max. Not just to share the news, but she'd need biker background and who better to provide it? Without stopping to consider, she pulled out her phone and selected the contact she'd been itching to press all day.

Rats! No answer on Max's cell. She left a message and called the station where she learned he wouldn't be in that day. She left another message on his voicemail, semi-confident that he'd get back to her shortly.

Would he think she was being possessive or presuming too much about their relationship if she texted him? *Maybe.* Would she text a friend under similar circumstances? *She would.* Was she too old for these teenage insecurities? *Absolutely.*

She kept the text light, breezy, and most of all, friendly.

*Congrats on good press for Mercer deal. Need background info for new project on motorcycle clubs. Since you're so awesome good, thought you might be willing to help. Call when you get a chance.*

There. That should do it.

She crossed her fingers and waited.

# Chapter Twelve

"The job's mine if I want it, Dad," Max said into the phone from his New York hotel suite. He tugged his tie off and tossed it aside. "They offered me a contract this afternoon."

"Are the terms good?"

"Better than I expected."

"Fantastic!" His dad's smooth, rich voice conveyed encouragement from Tennessee to New York as surely as Kenny Chesney could carry a tune. "All your dreams are coming true, son. I'm so proud of you."

"That means a lot to me." But then, Max had known his dad would feel that way. He'd pushed himself to accomplish his goals for his dad's sake as much as his own. Subconsciously, he might have hoped to prove to his dad that the sacrifices the man had made for his kids all these years had been worth it. "I've worked toward this moment for a long time." And now that he'd achieved it, the accomplishment left him feeling oddly flat.

"Yep. It's sure been a long road from a sixteen-year-old doing an internship at the local PBS station to Investigative Reporter on *Sixty Minutes*." From his dad's intonation, Max imagined the news show's name in all caps. "Nobody deserves it more than you." His dad chuckled with unmistakable delight. "But what I'm wondering is why you aren't out celebrating the news of a lifetime, instead of talking to your old man on the phone."

Max rubbed his hand over the tense muscles in the back of his neck and admitted the truth. "I guess because I haven't entirely decided to take the job." He cleared his throat and waited through a few seconds of stunned silence on both sides of the line. "What if I didn't? Would you be disappointed?"

"I'd never be disappointed in anything you did, son. You'd have to have a damned good reason or you wouldn't even consider turning the offer down."

Annabel flashed through his head with the brilliance of a lightning bolt. Stunned, Max dropped onto the edge of the bed, his mind reeling.

*No! No!* That couldn't be it. She couldn't be the reason for this atypical hesitation. Women were a disposable commodity. Easy come, easy go. Move in for the kill, then move on before they knew what hit 'em.

Or that's the way it had always been before, anyway.

Before Annabel.

For all the differences between them, Annabel was the first and only woman he'd known that he could picture growing old with. Her cautious instincts clashed with his wilder tendencies, but frankly, he'd outgrown his more outrageous stunts anyway. And he'd be happy to help Annabel shed more of her inhibitions and grab hold of some excitement. Should make for an interesting combination. Between them, they'd create a perfect balance.

"Well, Dad, what would you say if I told you I'd met this woman...?"

After another moment of stunned silence, his dad let out a loud whoop! "Hallelujah! 'Bout damn time."

The airplane returning Max to Cincinnati touched down late Friday morning. Even with everything going his way, between the case and the network contract, he'd barely had time to breathe since he'd left town on Sunday. He'd grown increasingly edgy as the week wore on.

He broke from the jetway at a trot with his duffle bag slung over his shoulder. Jogging to passenger pick up, he climbed into Roger's TV van before it rolled to a complete stop.

"You in a hurry there, bud?" the cameraman asked, swinging into traffic.

"You could say that." Max stowed his bag behind the seat and fastened his seatbelt. "I have a crapload to do before Tess's show this afternoon."

Roger raised an eyebrow. "I thought you big network stars had minions to do your bidding. You should be able to just sit back and let things flow now, shouldn't you?"

Max mentally reviewed the list of things to be accomplished in the next few hours. "I guess."

"Didn't they offer you everything you wanted?"

"I thought they did, but there's something missing." He pulled out his cell phone and entered Annabel's number.

Things had really looked up career-wise for her while he was out of town, too. She'd left him messages all over the place about her career opportunities. She even texted him, which he knew would have been a test to her courage.

With so many things to discuss, he hadn't wanted to do it over the phone, but he could hardly wait any longer. He'd planned to spring all this stuff on her in person this afternoon, but it might be better to talk to her first and prepare her for the surprises ahead.

Instead of Annabel Live, he got Annabel Pre-Recorded. He listened to the end of her prompt about leaving a message. After a few seconds of hesitation, he stumbled disjointedly through one. Damn. He should have prepared that better.

"Missing? Like what?" Roger asked when Max stowed the phone in his messenger bag. "You mean the network wouldn't come through with your own private plane? The cheap bastards. I thought the timing of the grand larceny case along with your action-figure derring-do would let you write your own ticket."

"It did." His stomach still cramped when he thought of Annabel risking her neck in such a volatile situation, but their face-to-face wrestling match with Swifty had netted him the right amount of publicity at just the right time. "You were pretty damned indispensable, too."

"Thanks, but I wouldn't want to haul ass over rooftops every day." The cameraman slid him a look. "Tell me about the new job."

"Fantastic pay, great schedule, enormous creative latitude," he told Roger, saving the best for last. "If I take it, they even agreed to let me hire my own team. You know any resourceful shooters who're interested in moving to the big time?"

Roger's double take sent the van veering into the next lane. "Any shooters? Like me?"

"That's right. What do you think?"

The cameraman mulled it over while they crossed the bridge into the city. "Nah, I couldn't leave Cincinnati."

The response had Max scratching his head. "Why not? The work will be challenging, and the money's good. And it's network, man."

Roger looked embarrassed. "Me and Ginger are kind of

serious. I've been thinking about settling down, maybe even starting a family."

"They allow families in New York, too, you know."

"Do they now? And how would you know?"

"It's something I've been thinking about myself."

"You kidding me?" With another sharp swerve to the right, Max held his breath while they almost sideswiped a semi before Roger returned the van to his own lane. "Mad Max Williams settling down? How long have you been thinking about this?"

"Awhile." Only ten or twelve hours, but Roger didn't need to know that. Max wasn't all that comfortable with the details himself yet. Go figure.

This morning, instead of signing on the dotted line, he'd asked for a deadline extension, because he knew he couldn't leave Cincinnati if that meant leaving Annabel, too.

"Which brings us to why I asked you to pick me up. I need another favor."

By Friday, Annabel's spirit had sagged down around her ankles like granny panties with a snapped waistband. Max, the rat, hadn't bothered to call her back. Or he hadn't bothered to leave any messages on her voicemail if he had. On Monday, he'd sent one cryptic text that left her edgier than ever. *In NYC. Crazy busy. Surrounded by suits. Lots to talk about when I get back. C U then. Take care.*

Really? *Take care?* Was that the best he could do? Wasn't that something he'd say to his niece or his sister or his grandmother? Was that his way of distancing himself from her? Telling her she wasn't important to him?

She'd spent more time fretting over and decoding Max's text than she'd spent considering her own life and career opportunities. Of course, she couldn't make up her mind between the LA offer or the biker video. She wanted to do them both, but neither one seemed just right.

Nothing about either decision hinged on Max Williams. She didn't need him. Not for her motorcycle piece, not for her peace of mind, not for anything. She wanted him, yes. She loved him, yes. But life would go on without him. Not happily, but then, when had that ever been an option?

She shouldn't be disappointed at the way things had turned

out. She was the one who'd set the rules when he left her the other night. She just hadn't expected him to follow them. Unless it suited him to do so. And it must have suited him not to call her. If she had to start getting over him, she could damn well start today.

Maybe he wouldn't even show up for the taping. That would be the ultimate humiliation, but she wouldn't let it show. She'd keep her head high, her hands steady, and her eyes dry. And her heart hidden under lock and key.

So fine. Returning from another unproductive meeting with Howard and more vague responses to his request for details on her new project, she picked up her phone to obsessively check for messages or texts from the elusive Max. And of course, there was one that had been left an hour ago right after she went to Howard's office. Just her luck. Damn Howard and his no-cell-phones-during-meetings policy.

Holding her breath, she listened to Max's message, thrilled to hear his voice again. I'm back in town. Hoped to talk to you before this afternoon, but maybe it's better if we don't. Have been strangely turned on by omelets and trench coats all week. I blame you for that. See you soon.

Her breath whooshed out. Okay, that sounded good. Probably. Mostly. At least she now knew he planned to show up to recap their dates. And that omelets and trench coats reminded him of her. In a good way. She could live with that. But how could it be better if he didn't talk to her before the show? That sounded a tad ominous. Maybe.

By the time she arrived at the station and deposited herself in the makeup chair for Voila, the manic elf, to transform her from drab to dazzling, Annabel was on the edge. She perked up her ears when she heard Max and Roger's voices in the hall. Giddy relief erased her anxiety.

"Did you give Tess's producer the new video?" Max asked.

"Sure did," Roger rumbled. "Everything's all set."

"Thanks for your help, man."

"My pleasure." The cameraman chuckled. Annabel heard them exchange slaps on shoulders, that masculine substitute for a hug. "In fact, I'm gonna stay for your segment."

"You don't have to do that."

This time Roger burst out in a full-bellied laugh. "I've been waiting for this for a long time. I wouldn't miss it for the world."

Annabel's nerves pinched tighter than her new shoes. Despite Max's preference, she'd be more relaxed if she had a private word with him before their on-air meeting. When Voila finished fluffing her hair, Annabel took a deep breath, removed her cape, and started to open the door.

"Max, darling!" a sultry voice crooned.

Annabel paused with her hand on the doorknob and stayed out of sight.

"Hey there, Tess."

"I hear congratulations are in order!"

Annabel's stomach turned over as she listened to a lip-smacking kiss. Her heart lurched at the confirmation of Max's departure from Cincinnati.

"And you're going to make the announcement on our little show," Tess continued. "I'm so honored."

Maybe jealousy over Max's success was the reason for Tess's catty tone.

"Well, don't be. This whole thing might blow up in my face." He sounded much more nervous, much less confident than she'd ever heard him.

"Not a chance," Tess purred.

"Is Annabel here yet?"

"Don't know. Let's find my producer and check."

Swallowing her disappointment, Annabel peeked out. Tess tucked her hand cozily around Max's arm, and they disappeared into a room down the hall.

"Anna!" Carly rushed up from the other direction. "Ohmygosh, I'm so sorry. Last time, you were almost late. This time, it's me. The traffic from school was terrible. You look fabulous in that color. Are you ready? Was that Max going in the opposite direction?"

Annabel laughed at the breathless exuberance. "Relax, you have plenty of time." She struck a model's pose and turned from side to side to show off her clingy new dress. "I'm glad you approve of an outfit I picked out for myself for a change. Yes, I'm ready, and yes, that was Max."

Carly's continued chatter settled Annabel's jitters better than a tranquilizer. The routine this time seemed almost familiar as she waited to take her turn in front of the camera. She marveled over how her life and feelings had altered in the two weeks since their first on-air appearance.

She supposed due to Max's celebrity status and coming announcement, their "date review" was scheduled as the final segment of the program. In the green room, she fidgeted through video reports and live post-mortems on the other couples' hits and misses. But almost before Annabel knew it, she and Carly took the stage.

"So," Tess began, grinning broadly. "Tell us how things went with you and Max."

Annabel wouldn't admit she'd fallen in love with someone who was leaving the city and didn't love her back, but she couldn't pretend there'd been no attraction, either. She offered up a carefully prepared neutral comment. "I'd say we hit it off pretty well."

"Great! That means we're 'pretty' good matchmakers, doesn't it, Carly? Let us in on the details about the first date, Annabel. Where did you and Max go? What did you do? And most importantly, how did it end?"

"We had a wonderful dinner at Ernesto's. Afterward, we went to the symphony at Music Hall. We didn't have very much in common, but Max turned out to be a lot nicer than I expected."

"Nicer?" Tess repeated on a laugh. "You went out with Max Williams and thought he was *nice?*" She raised her waxed eyebrow at the studio audience. "I know Max pretty well myself, and it must have been a low blow to his ego if you thought he was just nice. Most women think he's great, sexy, exciting, gorgeous, or the most wonderful man they've ever met."

Annabel wanted to thunk the talk-show queen in the head with her imaginary tiara. What did Tess hope to accomplish with this line of questioning? She hadn't grilled the other guests this way. "He's some of those things."

"And what about the end of the evening? You didn't tell us if you kissed."

"We shared a friendly kiss." Annabel feared that Tess would probe past Annabel's comfort zone if she didn't disclose at least that much.

"Let's watch and see." Tess pointed to the monitor. "Here's what Annabel and Max's date looked like."

It hurt Annabel to relive Max's arrival on her doorstep, to see how utterly endearing he looked over dinner and how sweet he'd been about escorting her to Music Hall. Her cheeks burned when the video got to their kiss! Their good-night kiss, the hot, carnal one she had told Roger absolutely not to use, played out for all to see.

The audience loved it and so did Tess. "You call that friendly?" she asked, and everyone laughed.

Annabel laughed along with them. What else could she do? "Well, that's friendlier than I remember it."

"Let's see how Max remembers it. Come on out, Max."

Annabel's heart pounded as Max came on stage as directed. She would carry this off with aplomb if it killed her. She crossed her legs and adjusted the hem of her dress. She'd slept with him the last time they'd met, sure, but no one else knew that. It wasn't as if she'd been assigned a scarlet letter.

Tess kissed him on the mouth, and he pecked Carly's cheek. Then, he kissed Annabel's hand. The remote, formality of the gesture left her cold, but the extra little squeeze he gave her fingers sent heat waves zinging straight to her heart. The accompanying look he gave her was hot enough to melt rock and bold enough to strip her naked.

He pressed a lacy bouquet of violets into her hands, and winked a silent message that gave her more hope than she'd had all week. "Why didn't you call me, damn you?" she wanted to shout, but pressed her lips together instead. They'd have time to talk privately later. She'd make sure of it.

Tess patted the chair farthest away from Annabel's for Max to sit in. "Now, tell Tess all about it, Max," she began as if the two of them were sharing private confidences over a drink. "What did you think of your first date with Annabel?"

"It was boring as hell." He directed his mega-watt smile straight at the camera. "I hate quiet dinners, I'd never been to the symphony, and letting a guy follow me around on a date with a camera practically guaranteed nothing steamier than hand-holding."

Of all the nerve! The old Annabel would have shrunk from the unfavorable review, but even with her heart nearly breaking, the new Annabel prepared words of retaliation.

"That's pretty harsh," Tess interjected, sliding Annabel a sly look. "Was the date a complete bust from your perspective?"

"It sounds like it, doesn't it?"

"Yes, but we saw the footage. There were enough sparks flying between the two of you to light up the sky over the river on Labor Day weekend."

"There sure were," Max drawled. "And that's when I realized, if we were generating that much heat on what had to be the world's worst date, what would happen if Annabel let her hair down?"

"Did you find out?"

"See for yourself."

The monitor revealed another montage of shots. Annabel and Max clinking champagne glasses. Annabel and Max on the Harley. Max flying out of the swing and into Max's arms. Annabel and Max kissing in the field behind the Blue Moon. Annabel and Max entering the award ceremony arm in arm. Annabel and Max tackling their assailant on Saturday night.

She couldn't believe how good she looked, how alive, how perfectly suited to Max. Whatever happened next, she had to get a copy of this video. She'd never again let herself or anyone else dismiss her as lackluster and boring!

Next came a shot of Max alone, dressed in jeans and a denim shirt, relaxing in a chair behind a desk in a cluttered office.

"Until two weeks ago, this," the digitally-recorded Max gestured around the room at the awards and photographs, "represented the most important part of my life. I wanted recognition for my work, the respect and the admiration of my peers, and the financial reward I thought I deserved." The camera followed as he moved to stand in front of his desk. "For the past few years, Annabel Morgan was nothing more than an annoying blip on my peripheral radar. I'm willing to acknowledge she both intrigued and irritated me, mostly because she found me so completely resistible. When fate and her stepdaughter threw her in my lap, I almost threw her right back."

Annabel's fingernails cut into her palms as he continued, terrified about what his words might or might not mean.

"Like most guys, I'm dumb as a stump when it comes to women, so it took me a little while to figure it out. By the end of our arranged date, I no longer had a choice. I couldn't live without her now if my life depended on it. And I think it does." He smiled then, and through the camera's lens, he looked directly at her, love shining in his eyes. "Annabel, I've never said this to anyone who wasn't already related to me, but I love you. I want to spend the rest of my life with you, showing you the endless ways in which we're exactly right for one another. What do you say to that, sweetheart? Want to take a ride on the wild side with me?"

The studio audience oohed and aahed. Somewhere in the background, Carly squealed with delight. "Yes!" she crowed, pumping her fist. "Way to go, Max! Go for it, Anna!"

Tears stung Annabel's eyes. Her heart pumped hard enough to burst through her ribs. Too stunned to make much sense of Max's declaration, she lifted her hand to her lips, afraid she'd misinterpreted the whole thing and would blurt out a string of nonsense.

Max *loved* her? Since when? While the audience and Max waited in hushed silence, her mind twisted the words inside and out looking for hidden meanings.

"Stay tuned," Tess broke in as Annabel continued to sit in stunned silence. "We'll find out what Annabel thinks after this commercial break."

Max rushed over and dropped to his knees beside her, his face creased into lines of concern. "Annabel? Honey? You all right? Get her some water or something," he said to a shadow off-stage. He brushed her cheek with his fingertips. "I didn't mean to put you on the spot. I just wanted to surprise you. Annabel? Say something, darlin'. I'm about to have a heart attack here."

"But—But—What about your job?" she managed to say. "I thought you were moving to New York."

"If it comes to a choice, I'd rather have you than the job. I'll stay here or I'll move to New York or LA or I'll commute if I have to. We can live anywhere that works for you." He dug around in his pocket and pulled out a blue velvet jeweler's box. "I've even got a ring."

She stared from the ring box to him and back again. "You're saying you want to get married?"

"Whatever it takes, Anna-honey. Whatever you want."

Finally, finally, she dared to believe. She thought about the proposal for about five seconds and made her decision. "Spell it out, Max. I want to hear you say it."

"I love you." He swallowed hard, his Adam's apple bobbing. "I want to get married." He held onto her hands like he was an astronaut floating in space and she was his lifeline to the mother ship. "Will you marry me?"

She could have left him dangling, but he looked so anxious, so serious, and so un-Max like, she didn't have the heart. "Yes."

He let out a whoop before the word was out of her mouth. He jumped up and pulled her into his arms, then he swung her around in an embrace that left them both breathless as the audience cheered. With the cameras rolling again, Carly and Tess joined them in a ferocious hug that included laughter and tears and rounds of "I told you so."

"I love you," Max said in her ear. "But I haven't heard those words from you yet."

She smiled, putting all her feelings into the look before she spoke the words. "I love you, too."

"Then hang on with everything you've got, honey. We're in for a wild ride."

With that promise, he pulled her into a scorching kiss that became the finale of *Let's Talk*'s promotional loop for the next decade.

# EPILOGUE

*Four years later...*

Two o'clock in the afternoon, and all Annabel wanted was a nap. But, no. Shifting in the sleek ergonomic marvel Max had insisted on buying for her, she tried to focus on Derek, her laid-back assistant. He sprawled, stretched out, full-length on her office sofa.

"I'll work up the changes we've talked about." Derek's multiple piercings, tattoos, and striped blue and black faux-hawk might lead the uninformed to doubt the talent and dedication he applied to their work, but Annabel knew better. "I have some ideas about punching up that first section with DeSean in the music studio. And that scene at the end, when the sunrise is coming through the windows? Backlighting DeSean? The shading should be more golden. I want the sound mixer to play with the music there some more, too."

"Right, we have the sound fading away, but let's see if there's more impact with it coming up instead, kind of bold and hopeful." The documentary on the independent music scene they'd been working on for the past year had all the earmarks of success. But the element Annabel liked most about the project was that it had been inspired by, and prominently featured, DeSean Daniels, one of her boys from *Challenging Destiny*. Absently, she typed in a couple more notes and saved them to their edit folder. "Can you have the changes completed by Monday?"

He nodded. "No problem, boss. I'm knocking off early today to get to out to Riverbend, but I'll make up the hours tomorrow or Sunday."

With an edgy style like a long music video with documentary content interspersed, *Making New Music* was the first film she'd produced solely for LuckyLady, the production company she'd started after leaving her apprenticeship with Lance Foreman. She felt a lot of pressure to get it right, not all of it self-imposed. Expectations ran high in film circles due to the Independent Filmmakers award hanging on her wall for *Rolling Thunder*, the documentary she'd made on motorcycle clubs while working under Lance's supervision. He'd taught her a lot, but she didn't want the film community thinking she couldn't produce the same kind of quality product on her own.

"I'm taking off for now, too." Too tired to do anything more for the day, Annabel started shutting down her computer and straightening things on her desk. "Enjoy the concert tonight."

"Right, you have fun in Columbus this weekend." Derek stood up from his couch-slouch and headed out of her office. "And tell Max thanks again for the concert tickets."

Still sitting at her desk, trying to summon the energy to move, she heard footsteps stop outside her door. She looked up, expecting Derek to have returned with one final thought. But the body filling her doorway with his trademark swagger and broad shoulders belonged to her handsome husband.

"Hey, pretty lady, want to go for a ride?" For the past twenty-four hours, he'd been traveling home from a grueling two-week detail in Afghanistan. He had to be bone weary, but right now he was looking at her like he was a starving man, she was a steak dinner, and he was ready to eat her up.

"You're home!" Even after three years of marriage, she couldn't help throwing herself at him the moment he walked through the door. So far, he'd always been happy to catch her. This afternoon was no exception. "I was afraid you'd be late."

"Told you I'd be here on time." He wrapped his arms around her and pulled her close, ducking his head to kiss her hello. "God, you feel good."

The fact that their two careers had them splitting their time between Cincinnati and New York, and Max was frequently away on assignment, meant they weren't always in the same place at the same time. Whenever possible, they traveled together. Sometimes she free-lanced for his team, sometimes he free-lanced for hers.

After she had completed her internship with Lance Foreman, she and Max had gotten married at a small ceremony at The Conservatory, with just family and close friends. Annabel had sold the house she and Carly had lived in, buying a three-story warehouse near downtown with Max.

They'd renovated the entire first floor into an office, studio and editing rooms for LuckyLady Productions. Their living quarters took up the second floor, making it easy for her to work whenever she needed to.

A darling efficiency apartment made up the third floor for Carly. Her hectic college schedule didn't allow her much time to visit, but when she did, she knew she always had a place to call home.

So far, the arrangement had worked out well, but Annabel could see more changes in their future. They'd have to find a way to add a nursery to the second level sometime soon, and maybe, look for a bigger apartment in New York

"But sometimes you run late." Gripping his shoulders, she jumped up and wrapped her legs around his waist.

"Not when I can help it." He linked his arms around her hips to hold her in place and kiss her again. Longer this time. With more tongue. "And not when we've got something this important to attend. It's not every day Carly graduates from OU at the top of her class."

"Pre-med, no less. She's one smart girl." She kissed him back and pointed up the stairs. "To the bedroom."

"Good idea." He smiled, turning to let her kill the lights on the studio level. "That's where I was headed."

"Because my suitcase is there?"

"Because I haven't seen you for ten days, and I want you so much even my eyeballs hurt." He nuzzled her neck, and she melted a little. "We don't have to leave this minute, do we?"

She laid her head on his shoulder and reveled in the pleasure of having him carry her up the stairs. "We do if we want to get there in time for the reception and dinner with Carly and her friends."

"Are you sure you aren't too tired to drive to Columbus tonight?"

"You'll be driving." She stifled a yawn. "I'll be sleeping most of the way."

He grazed his fingertips across her tummy. "Wouldn't you and the Peanut rather go to Columbus in the morning?"

She sniffed. "The Peanut and I don't want to get up that early."

By now, he'd reached the landing to their upstairs residence. Before opening the door, he nibbled his favorite spot in the crook of her neck, sending little goose bumps spiraling. "How have you been feeling?"

"Super, most of the time. Morning sickness only strikes occasionally, when it's least convenient for me." She pulled back to look at him. "Don't let the word morning fool you into thinking it can't occur any time. I'm hoping it won't hit during Carly's graduation ceremony tomorrow."

Just then, Carly's ringtone, "Matchmaker, Matchmaker," erupted from the phone in Max's back pocket. "Speaking of our graduate, can you reach around and get that?"

"Would you rather let it go to voicemail and call her back when we get on the road?"

"She's texted me twice already, worried I'd get stuck in New York due to all the storms on the coast. We should let her know I'm here."

As always, Annabel was touched at how sweet he was about Carly's place in their lives. Annabel knew it was partly because he genuinely liked her stepdaughter, but he'd admitted more than once that the girl would always have a special place in his heart for getting the two of them together.

Smiling, she pulled the phone from his pocket, slid her finger across the screen and punched an icon. "Hey, Carly. I answered Max's phone. You're on speaker, so you've got us both."

"Great! Max made it home all right?"

"Right on time," Annabel told her. "We're packing up and getting ready to leave in a few minutes."

He wasn't even breathing hard by the time he shouldered his way into their bedroom. It was bright and sunny and the bed looked soft and inviting. He laid her down amid a stack of pillows in the center of the billowy duvet. Keeping his gaze firmly fixed on Annabel, he pulled his t-shirt over his head, revealing the sculpted expanse that still managed to take her breath away. "I know we've got the big bash Anna's throwing you tomorrow, but what's the schedule for tonight, kiddo?"

"Schmoozing over cocktails with the faculty at six. Dinner at seven."

Max stretched out next to Annabel on the bed, lifted her shirttail, and rubbed his palm over her mostly non-existent baby bump. "Is cocktail hour mandatory?"

"No, but you should allow extra time for traffic. There are

so many visitors in town for commencement weekend, it's a zoo here."

"I can manage the traffic, but I'm a little concerned about Annabel."

"Concerned? Why? What's the matter?"

"I'm fine," Annabel interjected, punching Max's arm for worrying Carly.

Max's voice rode right over her. "She looks tired. I don't think she got enough rest while I was gone."

"My guess is she worked non-stop all week to get her editing finished before you got home and had to drive here for the weekend."

"She probably did!" Max nibbled on Annabel's ear.

"I did not!" Just to pay him back for distracting her, she tweaked his nipple. He liked it, so she tweaked the other one.

"Anna, it's vitally important for you to get plenty of rest during your first trimester." Carly didn't start medical school until the fall, but anyone listening to her would think she was already a trained professional. "Didn't you read the pregnancy materials I sent you?"

She bit her lip as Max unbuttoned her shirt and admired the new fullness of her breasts. He traced the soft flesh above her bra with his tongue. "Yes, Dr. Bossy, I did read them."

"She should rest now, Max, before you hit the road."

Max looked up at Annabel and winked. "You really think so?"

"I do," Carly confirmed. "I'll see you tonight whenever you get here."

"We'll be there in plenty of time for dinner," he assured her. "But we might miss the cocktail hour."

"That's all right," Carly said. "Annabel needs her rest more than she needs to stand around drinking tonic water with a bunch of stuffed shirts."

Kissing his way down Annabel's stomach he paused to say, "Thanks for understanding. We'll see you later, kiddo."

"Love you, guys. Bye!

"Love you, too, sweetie." Annabel disconnected the call and tossed the phone toward the bedside table. "That was bad. You shouldn't have done that."

"Bought us some time, though, didn't it?" He unzipped her jeans and slipped his hand inside her panties, finding her wet and ready for him. "You heard what Carly said. You have to rest."

She returned the favor, unzipping him and cupping his hard heat. "Somehow, I don't find this a bit restful."

"You will," he predicted, tossing her jeans aside. "You'll be longing for a nap after I've loved every inch of you."

"Will you stay with me while I rest?" she asked, thinking he needed sleep more than she did.

"You can count on it." He settled between her thighs, kissing her long and hard. "Always."

# Thank you!

Thank you for reading my debut novel, *Meet Your Mate*! I hope you enjoyed it as much as I enjoyed presenting it to you.

You may also enjoy *Cursed by Love* and *Meant for Me*, the second and third books in the Good Riders series, and *Happy This Year*, a Good Riders Christmas novella ebook. *Face the Music*, another Good Riders book is coming soon.

For information about when future books by me will hit the bookshelves, please visit www.jaciefloyd.com and sign up for my newsletter. Signing up for the newsletter will automatically enter you into a monthly drawing for a book giveaway.

My author page can be found on Facebook at https://www.facebook.com/JacieFloyd.

I can be followed on Twitter at: https://twitter.com/jaciefloyd

After reading a book, the two most important actions you can take are to recommend the title to friends and write a review of the book at Amazon, GoodReads, and wherever you go to talk about books with friends. Good or bad, let your opinion be known.

# Acknowledgments

For many writers, their most important resource is the community of writers surrounding them. For me, this includes all of the inspiring and talented women of The Ruby-Slippered Sisterhood, The Pixie Chicks, The Lucky 13s, the Fivecorners, The Golden Network, and the members of OVRWA who go back with me all the way to the beginning of this crazy endeavor. I am so grateful to have all of these outstanding women in my world.

Special thanks to my daughter Sarah. I literally could not have accomplished this goal without your encouragement and technical expertise. You give me joy.

Thank you to my son Evan, for doing what he can to make my life more fun and keep me current.

I'd like to thank my families, both bloodline and in-law, for always providing me with a place to call home.

Additional thanks to my editor, Annie Oortman, my cover designer, Kim Killion of The Killion Group, my excellent Beta Readers, Annie Woerner and Sarah Patrick, Leslie Lynch for guiding me through the perils of self-publishing, and to Darcy Woods, for her creative brilliance on twitter tags.

Last and most importantly, I must thank my amazingly handsome husband, Goble, for sticking by me and encouraging the fulfillment of this dream. He is my hero, my love, and my partner for life.

# About the Author

Jacie Floyd writes contemporary romance, romantic comedy, and emotionally-rich stories about the kind of strong women and bold men you want to read about and know.

From the time she read her first Nancy Drew mystery, she's been an avid reader and writer in a variety of genres. After many years as a wife and mother with a nine-to-five job, the desire to create her own stories became her obsession. While polishing her craft as an unpublished author, she was honored to be named a six-time Golden Heart® Finalist and two-time Golden Heart® winner by the Romance Writers of America. Finally giving in to the inevitable, she abandoned her day job in order to self-publish the kind of stories she likes to read and write. She hopes you like them too.

Jacie is happy to connect with readers at www.jaciefloyd.com, on Twitter at https://twitter.com/jaciefloyd and on Facebook at https://www.facebook.com/JacieFloyd.